Stuckey's Legacy:

The Legend Continues

Lori Crane

Lori Crane

Lori Crane Entertainment
www.LoriCrane.com

This book is a work of historical fiction.
Some names, characters, places, and incidents are from historical accounts. Some names, characters, places, and incidents are products of the author's imagination.

ISBN 978-0-9903120-1-7
eBook ISBN 978-0-9903120-2-4

Table of Contents

December 31, 1911 11:59 p.m.	7
Death of a Maid	13
Who is She?	17
Two Months Earlier, October 1911	23
A Celebration	31
Keep It Quiet	39
In the Club	45
Penelope Juzan	51
Quail Hunting	53
A Day on the Game Preserve	57
The Grand Dining Room	65
The January Social	71
A Surprise Visitor	79
Break Down	87
Another	93
Cat and Mouse	97
Confession	106
Changing Tides	111
Shunned	117
Privacy	123
He's Back	129
Insult and Retribution	133
Island Uproar	139
Consolation	145
Jealousy and Murder	153
Police	161
Revenge	167
Kidnapped	171
Word from the Artist	173
Evidence	177
Luke	181
The Truth	185

The Curse   191
Levi's Demise   197

Author's Notes   203
About the Author   204
Books by Lori Crane   205

December 31, 1911 11:59 p.m.

"...five...four...three...two...one...Happy New Year!" the crowd chanted in unison and the orchestra began to play "Auld Lang Syne." Balloons fell from the ceiling and confetti was tossed from the mezzanine. It fluttered to the floor, covering couples who clung together on the ballroom's massive dance floor. Wine flowed and lovers kissed, and twenty-two-year-old Levi stood off to the side, sipping his champagne, observing the festivities with a mixture of apathy and loathing.

A gentleman in a crumpled tuxedo, heading toward the bar, staggered by him and nodded. Levi coldly nodded back, hoping the intoxicated man wouldn't stop to chat. He was here to observe and mingle, not to spend the evening listening to a slurring drunkard. It had taken him a decade to get into this elite circle and he wasn't going to let some sot spoil it. He downed the remaining liquid, plopped his empty champagne glass on the nearest table, and quickly moved across the room.

Following a magnificent dinner of pheasant and turkey in the Grand Dining Room, he had thus far spent the evening strolling around the luxurious Jekyll Island Club, chatting with people with familiar surnames—Firestone, Carnegie, Rockefeller, Vanderbilt. He introduced himself to them as Levi Temple, a business partner of the late Cornelius Bliss.

Temple wasn't his real name, though he had been using it for the last ten years. Most people in his hometown of Meridian, Mississippi, would remember him as Levi Stuckey, the boy who'd mysteriously disappeared following the hanging of his father from the iron rails of Stuckey's Bridge. His father was Thomas Stuckey. He wasn't Levi's real father, but when someone back in those days assumed he was, Levi never bothered to correct them. As a matter of fact, Stuckey wasn't that man's real name, either. He took it from one of his victims, a man named Carter Stuckey. Carter Stuckey had spent the night at Thomas's inn on his way to deliver a trunk to Vicksburg—a trunk full of gold. Not many visitors ever left that inn, especially visitors who carried great wealth. Carter Stuckey fit that description, meeting his demise for being a deliveryman. Thomas Stuckey never got to enjoy the gold he stole, though. He was strung up for murder before he even viewed the sparkling contents of the trunk.

Following Thomas's hanging, twelve-year-old Levi disappeared with the trunk. He took a horse and wagon and rode away from Meridian with the trunk, and he didn't leave a trace.

After he fled, he dropped the name Stuckey so he'd never be associated with Thomas, Carter, or the missing trunk of gold. He considered taking back his given name, but he didn't want to be linked to the sack of crap who owned that name, either. It had been so long since he'd used his real name, he could barely remember what it was. So, after a quick deliberation, he took the name of the only man he'd ever trusted, the sheriff of Lauderdale County—J.R. Temple. Yes, Temple was a good name, a good name from a good man. Levi always felt a tinge of remorse for disappearing and leaving Sheriff Temple to wonder what happened to him, but at the time he didn't have a choice. He deserved more in life than a stolen name and a tainted past with murderers, drunks, and whores. The gold could give him the future he wanted.

Since the moment he left Lauderdale County, Levi had spent every waking hour infiltrating the inner circle of high society, and as of tonight, he had finally arrived. So far, this seemed a very good place to be. He sipped imported sparkling champagne as he socialized with gentlemen in expensive tuxedos, beautiful women adorned with exceptional jewels, and even a few servants who scurried around catering to the social elite. Though he wasn't born into this circle, and he thought most of them idiots who were beneath him, he felt at home here. He was finally receiving the respect he deserved.

As the orchestra struck up a lively ragtime tune, Levi walked toward the patio door to step outside and get a breath of fresh air. His heels clicked on the marble floor as he passed velvet chaise lounges and crystal chandeliers. The leaded-art glass was a sight to behold and the classical details of the mansion were breathtaking. He would have a house this fine someday.

He found the patio alit with lanterns and

twinkling holiday lights, flanked by sweeping staircases that led down to the beach. The half moon shone brightly in the winter sky, and an ocean breeze rustled through his dark blond hair. He closed his eyes for a moment and enjoyed the gentle wind on his face. He took a deep breath of the ocean draft. It smelled like fresh linen hung on the line. He opened his eyes and looked around. Baskets filled with late-blooming roses were spaced intermittently around the cement patio. Other than the fragrant flowers, he found the patio nearly empty. Everyone was inside on the dance floor celebrating the arrival of the new year. Everyone except that brunette he had been eyeing all evening.

He had noticed her hours earlier, the moment she entered the front door. She was petite but floated into the room like she owned the place, all willowy with a smoky air about her. Her charcoal-lined eyes were dark and seductive, hiding playfully behind the rim of her extravagant black velvet hat. When she walked, the long, white ostrich feather on top of her hat danced with each step. He found her movements intoxicating.

She wore the most luxurious mink stole he had ever seen, and when she removed it, she looked like a Grecian goddess. Her empire-waist dress flowed to the floor, the black velvet bodice cut low enough to make every man in the room stop and stare. The black fan she fluttered in front of her face made her even more exotic. Levi had attempted to approach her a few times throughout the evening, but she was always surrounded by admirers and he couldn't get close enough to utter a single word. Out here on the patio, she was again with a gentleman.

Levi stepped to the edge of the patio and placed his fingers on the railing. She had her back against the railing, being courted by some wealthy boy in a man's suit. Levi snickered. *These rich boys don't know how to seduce a woman*, he thought. *They think they can have anything they want, including a woman, simply because their fathers gave them money.*

He remained still and looked out to the sea. The moon illuminated a path of white on the dark water. The reflection went all the way to the horizon. He absentmindedly reached into his jacket pocket and pulled out his silver lighter. He flipped it open and closed over and over with one hand. He kept stealing glances to his left at the couple, wondering if he should interrupt them. The rich boy stumbled forward a little, almost falling onto the woman. He seemed to be more than a little drunk. Levi held his breath and waited for the woman to say something, hoping he'd be able to tell whether or not she needed him to intervene.

When she spoke, her voice had a deep rasp with the slightest Southern drawl. Why did that not surprise him? He felt a stirring in his loins and glanced again at the couple.

"Mr. Goodyear, I'm flattered by your attention, but don't you think we should be going back inside now? Your friends are surely looking for you."

The boy caught his balance, stood up straight, and countered, "No, they're not looking for me. They're having their own fun…just like we should." The boy leaned in for a kiss, but the woman turned her face to the left and looked directly into Levi's eyes. She smiled faintly.

It was not the plea of a woman needing assistance that he'd been expecting to see. The expression he saw on her face was one of confidence and power. This woman didn't need his help. She was more than capable of fending off a drunken suitor. Levi watched her as she scowled and playfully pushed on the boy's chest to back him away.

"Really, Mr. Goodyear, that's enough for now." She pushed harder on his chest.

The boy shrugged and mumbled something Levi couldn't make out. The woman pulled her fur around her shoulders and narrowed her eyes at Levi, suggesting he should mind his own business. She turned the boy toward the open doorway, tucked her arm into the crook of his elbow, and led him toward the ballroom. As the two made their way to the door, a woman's bloodcurdling scream came from the direction of the beach.

Levi and the couple turned toward the ocean, attempting to see the source of the screaming through the palm trees that lined the patio, but it was impossible. The screaming continued. People began streaming out of the ballroom, asking what was going on, and men sprinted down the stairs on both sides of the patio, hurrying toward the sound.

Levi turned and looked at the alluring woman, whose young suitor had left her standing alone while he joined the other men heading to the beach.

She stared into Levi's eyes with no expression.

Death of a Maid

When the crowd reached the beach, they found the screaming woman being held close by a man in a futile attempt to calm her. The pair stood next to the body of a young girl lying face up on the sand. The girl was wearing a black dress covered with a maid's white apron. Her head was cocked and her dark hair cascaded across the white sand. No bonnet lay nearby. Her lifeless eyes stared straight ahead. Her face was so pale; it was nearly the same color as the sand beneath her.

"Someone call a doctor," yelled the man holding the screaming woman, who was now crying.

"I'm a doctor," said one of the men as he made his way through the crowd toward the body. He knelt down and examined the maid.

"Is she all right?" another man asked.

The doctor shook his head. "No, she's not. She's dead."

"Dead? Well, what happened to her? What's she doing out here?" asked the man.

"Maybe someone dragged her out here," said the woman who had finally stopped screaming and crying.

"No, she would have been yelling as loudly as you if that were the case. This girl came out here on her own," the doctor said, rubbing the maid's neck.

"Should we carry her inside?" asked another voice in the expanding crowd.

The doctor looked up and said, "No, but you should see if you can reach the sheriff. There are strange markings on her neck. This girl has been strangled."

"Strangled?" The din of the crowd rose as people asked, "What did he say?" and others responded by repeating the doctor's statement. More partygoers arrived on the beach, asking what was going on. Women cried and men tried to peek through the crowd to get a better look. One woman fainted and some men carried her back inside. The scene grew chaotic as more and more people arrived.

A large, burly man with white hair and a handlebar mustache took charge of the scene and asked everyone to back up as to not disturb any evidence. He begged the guests to return to the ballroom, stressing that he and the good doctor had everything under control. The doctor said, "Thank you, Charles."

The large man nodded.

The doctor returned his attention to the girl. He closed her eyes with his hand and then looked up into the blackness of the ocean, his shoulders slumped.

Some doctor, Levi thought. He remained on the outskirts of the circle, vaguely listening to the orders given by the burly man and watching with only a mild curiosity. He was more interested in locating the woman in the mink stole. Somewhere between the patio and the beach, he had lost sight of her. He scanned the crowd, wondering where the object of his desire might have disappeared to.

He saw her on the other side of the throng of people. Moonlight shone on the white ostrich feather in her hat, while the ocean breeze ruffled her stole and made the feather dance wildly about. Strangely, she wasn't looking at the girl on the sand. She wasn't looking at the doctor or the ever increasing crowd of onlookers. She was staring at Levi. He gave her the slightest grin.

She scowled, put her head down, and marched back toward the mansion. He realized he'd probably offered his smile at an inappropriate moment. He watched her walk across the sand and glide up the stairs to the patio, and he reluctantly resisted his desire to follow her.

Who is She?

An hour later, Levi stood on the front steps of the club and watched the sheriff arrive with a handful of deputies in tow. Apparently when something happened in the world of the rich and mighty, the whole county was required to show up to investigate. The thought made him chuckle. These people thought they were so important; they had everyone else believing it, too. He watched the deputies scurry down to the beach to retrieve the body and the sheriff speaking with those in charge. More deputies were there than Levi had ever seen in one place at one time, but he didn't think there would be a lengthy investigation. He already knew all he needed to know about the maid—she had gone to the beach with someone who strangled her. What else did they need to investigate? Instead of listening to the sheriff ask questions about the girl and the night's events, Levi went back inside and wandered around the mansion, looking for the woman with the white ostrich feather.

A servant carrying a silver tray of champagne glasses passed him as he entered the main hallway. He grabbed a glass and continued into the ballroom. The orchestra was playing "Let Me Call You Sweetheart" and the charming melody filled the room. The dance floor was full with young lovers and drunken partiers. They apparently wouldn't allow the evening to end early because of the inopportune demise of a maid. Levi scanned the dance floor but didn't see the mysterious woman.

He returned to the entrance and spoke with the doorman. "Did the young woman in the mink stole with the white feather in her hat leave?"

"Miss Juzan? No, I don't believe she did, sir."

Levi nodded a thank you and continued his search, moving down the hallway to his left toward the billiard room. The ornately carved wooden double doors were open so he stuck his head in. He spotted her sitting on the edge of a billiard table covered in red felt. She was laughing, holding a glass of champagne, surrounded by three men who all had their backs to the door. Over their shoulders, she caught sight of Levi as he stood mute in the doorway. One of the men turned to see what she was looking at and locked eyes with Levi. Levi nodded and held up his glass in greeting but the man didn't respond. Instead, he turned back toward the woman and moved a couple inches to his left to block the line of sight between her and Levi.

Levi stood motionless for a few minutes, pondering whether to return to the ballroom and watch the dancers or pummel this guy's brains out right here, right now. He opted for the former.

Back in the ballroom, he stood next to the bar and watched the dancers. The drunken man in the crumpled tuxedo once again staggered toward the bar. Levi considered making a quick escape, but then again, drunks were good to pump for information.

"Good evening, sir. Happy New Year," Levi offered jovially.

"And to you, my good man," the white-haired man slurred.

"Are you having a good time tonight?"

"Sure. Booze, women, music—what's not to like?" The man nudged his glass toward the bartender, who was well aware of what to fill it with. The drunk's stomach was so large; the front of his vest touched the bar while he remained two feet away.

"Speaking of women, are you familiar with Miss Juzan?"

"Penny?" Spittle flew from the man's lips, landing on Levi's lapel.

Levi grabbed a napkin from the bar to wipe it off.

"Oh, I'm sorry," said the man. He also grabbed a napkin from the bar and attempted to help wipe Levi's lapel.

He stumbled forward and almost fell on Levi, but Levi caught him by the arm and said, "That's okay, chap. I have it. So, Penny's her first name?"

The man lost interest in Levi's lapel when the bartender placed a fresh drink on the counter in front of him. He grabbed it clumsily, sloshing some liquid onto the bar before carefully lifting it to his lips to take a sip. He then noticed his drink dripping onto his belly and held up the glass to look at it, puzzled.

"What about Penny Juzan?" Levi asked again.

"Oh, Penelope!" the man said. "She's a lovely woman."

"Where is she from?"

The man paused, staring with a wrinkled brow into nowhere. "I don't rightly know. I think her uncle is an art collector or something."

"Is she married?"

"Penny? Married? No, no. If she were married, she wouldn't always be surrounded by admirers."

The man had a point. Levi looked across the dance floor, wondering what his next move with this woman should be, and found himself looking directly into the eyes of Penelope Juzan. She was dancing with the man from the billiard room, glancing over his shoulder, watching Levi. She moved like a ballerina, slow and graceful. Levi recognized the orchestra's melody as "There Never Was a Girl Like You," which he found apropos for the moment.

As he was admiring her gliding across the dance floor, the old drunk next to him fell flat on his back. Levi bent down and tried to help him up, but the man was out cold, snoring almost as loudly as the orchestra was playing. The bartender waved down a few men and together they picked up the drunk and placed him on the nearest settee. By the time they got the man settled and Levi looked back at the dance floor, Penelope Juzan was gone. He searched the entire mansion for her, but to no avail. He decided to go talk to the doorman again.

He found the doorman outside, helping Penelope Juzan into a brand new Columbus Roadster. She looked up at Levi as he froze at the top of the steps. He watched her car pull away and disappear into the night.

"I didn't know there were any cars on the island," he said to the doorman.

"Oh, there are a few, but they don't get driven very much." The doorman pointed in the direction the roadster had gone. "That one belongs to Mr. Firestone. He keeps it on the island for nights like this when a donkey or wagon would be too inconvenient. Other than that, you don't see them very often."

I should get myself one of those roadsters, Levi thought. He nodded to the doorman and returned to the party.

Two Months Earlier, October 1911

At 5:00 a.m., Levi sat in a diner on the corner of Meeting and Battery, enjoying a steaming cup of black coffee. He had found his way to Charleston Harbor a few months earlier and liked the bustling energy of the place so he stayed. He sipped his coffee and opened a week-old copy of the *News and Courier*, which he had retrieved from a stack of newspapers near the front door of the diner. As always, he flipped toward the society page first. He viewed it as an encyclopedia of sorts, helping him keep tabs on the wealthy and powerful. However, as he scanned the pages, something in the obituaries caught his eye, and he stopped to read the name at the top of the page.

Cornelius N. Bliss, Merchant, Dies

Cornelius N. Bliss, merchant, Secretary of the Interior in President McKinley's administration, and Treasurer of the Republican National Committee in four successive campaigns, died last night at his residence, 29 East Thirty-Seventh Street, New York. The cause of death was heart disease, due in great measure to extreme age. He was 78 years old.

Mr. Bliss's health began to fail about a year ago. He spent the summer at his country home in Oceanic, NJ, but was so feeble that he was able to leave the house only a few times during the summer. He took one or two drives during August with Dr. Arthur W. Bingham of 266 West Eighty-Eighth Street, who was with Mr. Bliss constantly after his health gave way.

The article went on and on, describing how wonderful Mr. Bliss was and mentioning all the accomplishments he had achieved, but one thing above the rest captured Levi's attention. Not only did Mr. Bliss have a home in New York and a country home in New Jersey, he also had a winter home on Jekyll Island, which was off the coast of Georgia.

The Jekyll Island Club was the most prestigious resort on the southeastern seaboard. In most circles, it was casually referred to as the Millionaires Club. New York's high society usually spent summer in the Hamptons to escape the heat of the city and winter on Jekyll Island to escape the harsh, freezing temperatures. Levi had always wanted to be one of those people with vacation homes in different locations. During the winter season on Jekyll Island, the club hosted balls and galas in the evenings and hunting during the day, with restocked populations of quail, pheasant, and deer. Levi couldn't wait to participate in those kinds of activities.

In October of 1907, during the financial panic that was fueled by the drop of the stock market, the US government had been nearly useless in helping the people and completely inadequate in aiding the financial sector. It simply did not have the funds to help the ailing economy. People tried to pull their money out of local banks, but bankers didn't have the money to return to them, causing a nationwide crisis that saw people and businesses going bankrupt. Nelson Aldrich, a senator from Rhode Island, spent the next few years traveling to Britain, France, and Germany, studying their financial systems. It was rumored that in 1910, Senator Aldrich invited his cronies to a top-secret meeting on Jekyll Island to discuss the financial crisis and the possibility of creating a national banking system. Friends like J.P. Morgan and John Rockefeller had put their own money into the system to shore up the banks. They certainly didn't want to have to do that again, so word on the street was that with the new system, the federal government would have the ability and power to back the banks in a future crisis. Levi didn't know how they would go about doing such a thing, but with the vast treasure of gold he had in his possession, paper money didn't mean much to him and he didn't care to understand. He did, however, wonder why these rich men with their numerous homes all over the country would need to meet on the island all the way down in Georgia, and do so in secret. Maybe someday he would meet and ask them.

A few years before, Levi had looked into joining the prestigious Jekyll Island Club, but the door was closed in his face at every turn. Apparently one needed to know someone who was already affiliated with the club to obtain membership.

Since high-society men all knew each other, it was difficult, if not impossible, for Levi to infiltrate their circle.

He took another sip of his coffee and gazed across the harbor at the ribbons of first-morning light filtering across the sky. He felt the steam from the cup on his face as he pondered which residence on Jekyll

Island belonged to Cornelius Bliss, and he wondered if anyone would be staying there now. He knew the affluent traveled with their servants, so he figured Bliss's island residence would be empty since his staff was probably in New York. Perhaps Levi would pack his belongings and head to Jekyll Island to find out for himself.

The waitress plopped his plate of scrambled eggs down in front of him and asked if he wanted more coffee. He nodded.

He looked out the window again and watched the sky change from navy blue to light blue with the rising of the sun, and for a moment he didn't realize what he was looking at. An enormous steam yacht was blocking his view of the ocean. She was undoubtedly the largest ship he had ever seen. In the center of her main deck stood a giant black smokestack flanked by towering masts. Ropes draped every inch of her yards. Levi had never seen so many ropes. She had to be over two hundred and fifty feet long, a massive white goddess floating on the murky sea.

When the waitress reappeared with a coffee pot, he asked, "When did that yacht pull in?"

The woman followed his gaze out the window. "She arrived at sunset yesterday. Beauty, isn't she?"

"Certainly is. Who does she belong to?"

The waitress placed the coffee pot on the table and one hand on her hip as she stared out the window. "That's the *Liberty,* belongs to Joseph Pulitzer. He always sails by this time of year and stops in for a few days. Headed to Jekyll Island for the winter, I believe."

Jekyll Island? Levi thought this must be a sign. He didn't know what kind of sign, but a sign nonetheless. His decision was made—he was going to

Jekyll Island. He wondered if he should take the train down or befriend Mr. Pulitzer and travel by yacht. He smiled at the thought of lounging on the *Liberty's* magnificent decks as seabirds flew overhead and waves pounded her hull.

Over the next few days, he kept a close eye on the yacht but was disappointed that he never saw anyone coming or going. He couldn't imagine why someone would pull into a port and then never leave the ship. The newspaper headline on October 30th solved the mystery.

Joseph Pulitzer Dies Suddenly

Charleston, SC, Oct. 29—Joseph Pulitzer, proprietor of The New York World and St. Louis Post-Dispatch, died aboard his yacht, Liberty, in Charleston Harbor at 1:40 p.m. The cause of Mr. Pulitzer's death was heart disease. Although he had been in poor health for some time, there was no suspicion on the part of those accompanying him that his condition was so serious.

Mr. Pulitzer's body will be taken north at 4:30 p.m. on October 30th on a special Pullman car. The funeral will be held at Woodlawn Cemetery in New York toward the end of this week.

Well, so much for getting a ride to Jekyll Island. Levi pouted as he looked through the greasy diner window at the colossal yacht he had dreamed of sailing on.

At 4:00 p.m., he stood on the dock as seabirds squawked over his head and pecked around the ground looking for a morsel to eat. He watched the yacht staff carry Pulitzer's body down the gangway of the ship amid the sobs of his widow and his stoic adult sons who flanked either side of her. When the small crowd left, Levi strolled back and forth along the length of the ship, admiring her graceful lines. She certainly was a beauty. He wondered if she would now be for sale and how much her purchase price would be. He had never before considered procuring a yacht but the idea certainly appealed to him. Surely, with a vessel this beautiful, the Jekyll Island Club would have to offer him a membership. He decided to have a closer look at her come nightfall.

Later that evening, Levi watched the pier until everyone had gone home before he sneaked up the gangway and onto the deck of the *Liberty*. He eased his way to the back deck, where passengers would gather. It was covered with teak furniture with plush white cushions. Between two sofas rested a glass coffee table on a thick white rug. Atop the table sat two lanterns. Levi looked around; none of the lanterns on the deck were lit. He stood still for a moment and listened. He didn't hear anyone aboard, only the sound of whistling seabirds, wavelets lapping the hull, and the haunting creak of the ropes that secured the *Liberty* to the dock.

To his right was a closed wooden door that he believed led to the passenger cabins. He tiptoed over and placed his ear to the door. He heard nothing.

He grabbed one of the lanterns from the coffee table and slowly turned the doorknob. The interior was dark, with only a small amount of light coming through the porthole windows. He cautiously stepped down three steps, closed the door behind him, and lit the lantern. As the soft light flooded the room, he saw a red velvet sofa to his right, with matching chairs to his left. He had never seen a room so opulent. Bookshelves lined one wall, filled with first editions of masterpieces, and fine art hung between the porthole windows. He recognized some of the paintings. He pulled the thick curtains over the windows to make sure his lantern light wouldn't be witnessed from outside.

On the back wall hung a tapestry depicting youths playing on the lawn in front of a manor house. With his limited knowledge of art, Levi figured it was probably seventeenth century. Someday he would own one of those. Why would these people deserve such elegance and not him? He wondered how much the tapestry would cost to buy, and then he wondered if he could simply roll it up and take it with him.

In front of the tapestry sat a large desk that he assumed was Mr. Pulitzer's. He crept behind it, pulled out the leather chair, and sat down. He placed the lantern on the desk and rubbed his palms across the dark wood. It was as smooth as silk. Not only did he deserve the tapestry, he deserved a desk this magnificent to place in front of it. He leaned back in the chair, folded his arms, and looked about the room.

He pictured himself as its owner and wondered what it would cost to maintain a ship of this size. He figured there must be some receipts in the desk.

He pulled out a side drawer and saw endless sheets of paper. He removed the top few sheets and looked through them. They looked like rough drafts of stories with many lines crossed out and rewritten, some neatly, some scribbled. Well, a drawer full of articles and stories would make sense, considering Mr. Pulitzer was a newspaper publisher.

He replaced the papers, pushed that drawer back in, and pulled out the center drawer. Pens, pencils, erasers, keys, unopened cigars, and a silver lighter. He flipped the top of the lighter open and pushed the ignition button to light it. It was old but beautifully polished. The silver had a fish-scale design embossed on it. He had never seen anything like it. He flipped the top closed, tucked it into his jacket pocket, and continued to look through the contents of the drawer. He found an envelope. He picked it up, turned it over, and read it. It was addressed to Mr. Pulitzer and was from the Jekyll Island Club. Levi envisioned his name as the recipient and smiled. He leaned back in the chair, flipped open the flap, and removed the contents—a letter and two tickets. He unfolded the letter.

Dear Mr. Joseph Pulitzer,

You are cordially invited to the Jekyll Island Club's annual New Year's Eve Gala. Please find enclosed two tickets for the event on December 31, 1911. We look forward to the pleasure of your company for dining, dancing, and cocktails at seven o'clock in the evening. The attire is formal.

Sincerely,
Charles Lanier
President, Jekyll Island Club

Levi couldn't believe his luck. Finally, he would rub elbows with high society. He tucked the tickets in his pocket next to the silver lighter. He then extinguished the lantern and snuck off the ship.

A Celebration

Levi was so elated at his good fortune, he knew he wouldn't be able to sleep, so he stopped off at the King Street Pub near the old Charleston Orphan House. He wandered into the musty-smelling place, with its plank floor and wood tables, and ordered a whiskey at the bar. Ragtime music filled the room from a piano player in the corner, and the air was foggy with cigar smoke. He always thought he'd like to partake in the habit but he just couldn't stand the smell. He pulled the silver lighter from his pocket and flipped the top open and closed over and over without pushing the ignition button. He gazed around the room. The place was quite lively for a Monday night. A handful of men sat at the other end of the bar and a few played cards around a large table in the center of the room.

"Where are all the women?" he asked the barkeep.

"Not much business for them here on a Monday, but I can send for some ladies if you'd like."

The husky man wiped down the bar top with a dirty cloth and then shoved it back into his stained apron. "You'll have to make it worth their time, though, if you know what I mean."

Levi grinned. "I can certainly do that. I'm having a celebration of sorts tonight. It'd be nice to have some company."

"Louis!" the barkeep called over his shoulder.

Levi downed his drink as a dirty, young boy dressed in knickers, with long curls sticking out of his sailor hat, appeared from around the corner. The barkeep told him to run down to Miss Mabel's place and ask her to send over a couple ladies. The boy nodded and ran back the same way he had come.

The man turned to Levi. "They'll be here shortly. Miss Mabel runs a tight ship."

The word *ship* made Levi smile. He flipped the lighter open and closed again.

"Why don't you get in on a couple hands of poker and a good cigar while you wait," the barkeep said, gesturing toward the game.

"No, I'm not much of a card player and not really in the mood for a cigar. I'll just have a refill and wait for the ladies." Levi pushed his empty glass toward the barkeep, who refilled it and sloshed it back toward Levi.

Levi downed the whiskey and listened to the piano player for a few minutes. When the man started playing "Camptown Races," Levi started humming along. "Doo dah, doo dah, camptown racetrack's five miles long, oh..."

His singing was interrupted by the jingle of the brass bells on the front door. He spun around and saw two women enter. They glanced at the barkeep, who nodded toward Levi. One of the women was a buxom brunette, wearing a light green dress that gave her body more of an hourglass shape than she probably had. The other was a blonde, wearing a loose-fitting blue dress that sloppily drooped off one shoulder. She caught Levi's eye and dramatically pulled the neckline back up to its proper spot, raising her chin as if she were royalty and he a mere peasant. He smiled at her pompousness. Neither women wore a hat, which he found strange, as it was an obligatory fashion accessory these days, but both women had their hair pinned up in a respectable style.

"Hello," they said as they approached the bar and sat on either side of Levi.

"Hello, ladies. Would you care for a cocktail?"

They looked at the barkeep, and he nodded and walked away to get their drinks. Apparently this wasn't their first time here and the barkeep knew what they wanted. The man returned a moment later and opened a bottle of imported wine. Levi recognized the label and knew it to be expensive. He chuckled. These amateurs thought they could take advantage of him by spending all his money. Little did they know, he could buy all three of them *and* the pub and still have plenty of money left to do it all again tomorrow. And the next day.

"So, what are your names?" Levi asked, looking back and forth between the women.

The brunette spoke first. "I'm Myrtle and this is Grace."

"Well, Myrtle and Grace, shall we make a toast?"

They all held their glasses in the air.

"To new friends."

They drank. When they set their glasses back on the bar, Levi grabbed the half-empty bottle, pulled a gold coin from his pocket, and held both items out to Myrtle. "I'll tell you what, Myrtle. You are a lovely woman indeed, but I would like to spend some time alone with Grace here, so you can run along." He smiled while he waited for her to take the wine and the coin.

She looked at his hands, then his face, then back at his hands. At first she looked angry at being dismissed, but when he dropped the gold coin into her palm, her expression softened.

"Well, that will be just fine, Mr....um..."

"You can call me Joe, like Joseph Pulitzer who owns that big yacht in the harbor."

Myrtle was speechless. She remained on the barstool, holding the wine bottle and gold coin, unmoving.

"Thank you for coming, Myrtle," Levi said, encouraging her to leave.

Reluctantly she rose and walked toward the front door, her green skirt swishing with each step. She gave Grace a wink as she passed.

After a few drinks and laughs with Grace, who turned out to be a charming girl, Levi told her all about the Millionaires Club that he would soon join. After an hour, he flipped a couple gold coins on the bar, nodded to the barkeep, and escorted Grace out into the night.

The starlit night was perfect for a romantic walk, and it would have been pleasurable to stroll the streets for a while in the balmy night air, but Levi had more immediate plans for his escort. He marched her to the nearest hotel and checked in under the name Thomas Stuckey.

"I thought your name was Joe." The girl giggled as she entwined her arms in his.

"It is Joe, but I don't want to put that on the hotel register."

They kissed as they staggered up the stairs, laughing all the way up to their room on the top floor of the three-story hotel.

Following their lovemaking session, Grace lay in Levi's arms and listened to him tell her all about the fancy people he was going to be friends with on Jekyll Island, about Cornelius Bliss's death, and about the New Year's Eve Gala tickets he'd found when he broke onto Mr. Pulitzer's yacht.

She rolled over onto her stomach, crossed her arms across his bare chest, and looked at his face. Her blonde ringlets danced across her face and he softly pushed them from her temple.

"You're really quite pretty, you know that?"

She blushed. "Then why don't you take me with you?"

"Oh, that's out of the question, dear. I'm going to meet wealthy society people, and I don't think you'll fit in."

"Well, what makes you think you'll fit in?" she teased.

"Don't you think I'm one of them?" Levi frowned.

"Mister, I grew up in the Charleston Orphan House. I know a poor orphan when I see one."

"Well, I never lived at the Charleston Orphan House, but it's true I'm an orphan."

She looked at him like a lovesick schoolgirl and waited for him to elaborate.

"I was orphaned years ago. My father was a

drunk. He killed my mother right in front of me when I was eight years old."

Grace gasped.

Levi continued. "He strangled her after he caught her fooling around with a man from up the road. He murdered both of them in a fit of drunken rage." Levi looked away from her and stared at the ceiling.

"I'm sorry. You probably loved her very much, huh?"

"I don't know. I thought I did for a long time, but my father pounded into my head that my mother was not worthy of my love. She was a whore."

Grace grinned. "Well, I'm a whore. It's not all bad."

He looked at her with surprise. He didn't think of her like that, but it was true. "I guess you are, aren't you?"

"What happened to your father?"

"I killed him," Levi said flatly and looked back at the ceiling.

After a few uncomfortable seconds, Grace giggled. "No, really, what happened to your father?

He looked her in the eye. "I killed him."

He paused to watch her expression and was satisfied with the look of fear in her eyes. "The more I thought about what he had done to my mother and all the nasty things he said about her, the more I realized he deserved to die, so I killed him."

Grace sat up and reached for her dress at the foot of the bed. She slid it over her head as she said, "Well, I should be going now. Miss Mabel will wonder where I disappeared to."

As she started to stand up, Levi sat up and

grabbed her wrist.

She tried to pull out of his grasp. "Joe, let go of me! I have to go!"

Levi grabbed her around the waist and placed his hand over her mouth. "No, you're not going anywhere." He grabbed his brown leather belt from the floor, wrapped it around her neck, and pulled tightly. She tried to put her fingers between the belt and her throat and struggled for a few minutes, but she was no match for his strength. Within a few short moments, she was dead.

He placed her in the bed, covered her with the quilt, and said, "You didn't really think I'd tell you all of that and let you live to tell anyone, did you?"

He kissed her on the forehead and rose to dress. He left the hotel room, knowing by the time anyone found her body, he would be long gone. To Jekyll Island.

Keep It Quiet

Following Penelope Juzan's departure, Levi wandered around the mansion, searching for something or perhaps someone to occupy the rest of his evening. He strolled down the hall to the library and found the door closed. *That's strange. It was open before.* He tried the handle but the door was locked. He leaned his ear to the door and heard male voices coming from inside.

"Sheriff, we can't let this get out. There's no one on the island except our families and servants. Everyone's going to say whoever murdered that girl was one of us. We just can't have that kind of publicity."

The sheriff's gruff voice was recognizable. "I understand that, but I need to find out who did this, and her family will undoubtedly come looking for her at some point."

"Well, of course they will, but we can't have the press breathing down our necks in the meantime. We all have businesses to run and reputations to uphold."

"I respect that, sir. I'll tell you what, I'll

investigate here on the island, and I won't give the press any reports until we know more. I promise I'll find out who did this, and I'll keep it as quiet as possible until then. Is that all right?"

"We appreciate that, Sheriff."

"We sure do. No one here can afford to have their names dragged through the mud, especially over some servant girl."

Levi heard footsteps moving toward the door from the inside, so he quickly slipped down the hall. He peeked through a potted palm and saw three men emerge from the room. Levi recognized the sheriff but not the other two men. They were dressed well enough, but they were not the elite names he had met throughout the evening. The two men bid the sheriff good-bye and when he left, they remained in the hallway to continue their discussion. Levi couldn't hear them very well but heard them say something about "avoiding a scandal for the bosses" and assumed these men were assistants to the wealthier members. Levi had noticed throughout the evening that all the wealthy men were accompanied by assistants and partners.

That gave him an idea.

He left the mansion, waving a cheery good night to the doorman, and headed down the road. He passed partygoers staggering home from the night's festivities and a few carriages with sleeping horses and drivers who were still waiting for their passengers. He passed palm trees, moss-draped oaks, and rhododendron bushes as he shuffled down the sandy road toward the club's annex.

When he turned the corner and the building came into sight, it took his breath away. It was an enormous three-story building, almost larger than the club itself. Many of the windows on the upper floors were alit, and the landscaping, from what he could see in the dark, was well manicured, with palm trees and bushes strategically placed between the huge picture windows that surrounded the first floor. He knew from his research that the building consisted of six apartments on the first floor, eight suites on the second floor, and twenty sleeping rooms on the third floor that were reserved for servants. He'd also found out that apartment number one belonged to John S. Kennedy, who'd died two years earlier; apartment number three belonged to John Albright, who was at home in Buffalo stocking an art gallery he'd recently built; and, in between, apartment number two belonged to the late Cornelius Bliss.

Mr. Bliss's apartment would be perfect. There would be no neighbors on either side to bother Levi. He looked around and saw no witnesses to his arrival at the annex. He entered the hallway through the back door and found Mr. Bliss's apartment. He remained quiet and still for a moment, listening for other residents, but heard nothing. He pulled his pocketknife from his trouser pocket, broke open the lock, and entered the apartment.

Even in the darkness, he could tell the apartment was exquisitely appointed. He found the nearest lamp and clicked it on. The soft light brought to life the attractive furnishings and decorations. Thick curtains hung from the picture windows, a massive stone fireplace filled the opposite wall, a huge deer head adorned the chimney, and plush sofas and chairs covered the parlor. In front of the fireplace was a rug made from animal pelts, and next to it was a stuffed duck standing guard over a stack of wood and wrought-iron poker. Mr. Bliss had been an avid hunter.

It was quite chilly in the room, so Levi said *excuse me* to the duck as he reached behind it for some logs and filled the fireplace. He pulled out his silver lighter and lit the kindling, blowing on it a bit to get it started. The wood was so dry, it caught fire almost immediately. He stood in front of the crackling fire, rubbing his hands together.

"That's better, huh?" he asked the duck.

There was a rap on the door.

Levi froze and waited. Maybe the person would go away. A moment later, there was a second knock.

He took a deep breath, exhaled, and inched open the door.

It was the burly man with the handlebar mustache from the beach.

"Good evening, sir. I'm Charles Lanier, the president of the Jekyll Island Club. I just wanted to see who was here since I wasn't informed Mr. Bliss had offered use of his apartment to anyone."

Levi held out his hand. "Mr. Lanier, it's a pleasure to make your acquaintance. Cornelius, um, Mr. Bliss, mentioned you on many occasions. I'm his business partner, Levi Temple." Levi backed out of the doorway and gestured for the man to enter. "Won't you come in?"

Lanier shook his head. "Oh, no, no, it's too late for a visit. I just wanted to see who was here. I saw you at the party, but I'm afraid I didn't get a chance to introduce myself what with all the commotion on the beach."

"Oh, that's understandable, Mr. Lanier.

Cornelius said I could use his apartment anytime, and since his unfortunate demise, I figured no one else would be here, so I thought I'd get away from the city for a bit. I picked up the keys from his wife Mary and came down from New York just today. I don't know how long I'll be staying."

"Well, it's nice to have you here, Mr. Temple. Enjoy your stay." Lanier turned to walk away, and then turned back. "Some of the club members are meeting for breakfast at seven if you'd like to join us. I'd be happy to introduce you to the gentlemen if you don't know them."

Levi smiled and nodded. "That would be very nice. Thank you."

"Okay, then, we'll see you in the Grand Dining Room at seven."

"Thank you, Mr. Lanier."

"Please call me Charles."

"Very well, then. Good night, Charles."

"Goodnight, Mr. Temple."

"Levi, please."

Charles nodded and made his departure.

Levi gently closed the door and turned to the duck. "Well, that went well, don't you think?"

In the Club

Levi rose early and found a young servant boy raking leaves outside. He sent the boy to tell the ferry master to have Levi's belongings delivered to apartment two. When he arrived yesterday, he'd paid the boat driver a nice sum to keep his bags overnight and he hoped the man did as promised.

While he awaited his trunk and suitcases, he looked through the apartment and found wine in the wine rack and a full pantry in the back of the kitchen. He also conveniently found a key to the front door in the drawer by the stove. That would come in handy. He'd hate to break his knife on the door lock if he had to keep entering the building that way.

When his trunk and two suitcases arrived an hour later, he dressed for breakfast in his most expensive suit and tie. He put on his trousers and topped off his outfit with his favorite belt. He'd bought it the year before from a fancy store in New York and he loved it. It was the first frivolous purchase he had ever made. It was brown leather and had geometric lines and squares embossed on it. Levi thought it looked like some sort of Indian design. Until he bought it, he had always held his trousers up with a piece of twine like some poor hillbilly from Mississippi, but no longer.

He straightened his tie and combed his hair over and over, hoping a perfect tie and hair would make him fit in with this elite society. "Here we go," he said to himself as he closed the door of apartment two and headed down the hall of the annex.

He squinted into the sunrise as he emerged into the yard and looked around. The island was vastly more beautiful during the day than it had been last night. Seabirds sang, palm trees swayed in the ocean breeze, flowers bloomed, and bright white sand covered every crevasse available to cover. It was so white, it was almost blinding. From the amount of sand he had already found in the apartment, he figured he'd tire of it sooner or later, but for now, it was very pretty. He waved good morning to a few children who were playing croquet on the front lawn of the club, and he wiped a bead of sweat from his brow as he climbed the steps to the entrance. It wasn't very hot but it sure was humid. He wondered if that meant rain was on its way.

He was greeted by a doorman who was different from the man last night but dressed the same. "Happy New Year, sir. How may I direct you?"

"Happy New Year to you. I'm having breakfast with Mr. Lanier."

The doorman nodded and turned toward the Grand Dining Room. "Right this way, sir."

When they approached the dining room, the doorman said something to the maître d', who also said,

"Right this way, sir."

They strolled through the packed dining room, filled with more than two dozen tables, and just about every seat taken. The maître d' walked Levi right through the middle of the crowd to a large table near the back of the room. The table sat in an alcove, surrounded by very high windows, and the sunlight streaming through them sparkled on the sweating water glasses.

As Levi approached the table, he counted a half dozen men seated there and recognized all of their faces. Charles, at the head of the table, rose to greet him. He was wearing a casual beige shirt, beige sweater, beige trousers, and a huge smile. Levi politely nodded to the rest of the men, who were also dressed casually, and he instantly knew he was overdressed.

"Gentlemen, I'd like to introduce you to Cornelius's business partner, Levi Temple." Something caught Charles's eye across the room. "If you wouldn't mind, would you please introduce yourselves? I need to take care of something." He placed his linen napkin on the table and gestured for Levi to take the empty seat next to his, then patted Levi on the arm and left.

The men rose one at a time, shaking Levi's hand and introducing themselves—J.P. Morgan, John Rockefeller, Nelson Aldrich, Richard Crane, and James Hill. Levi was positive there had never been a table of more wealthy businessmen in the entire world, and he was pleasantly surprised they all seemed cordial.

"I'm very sorry to hear about Cornelius," said James as Levi settled into his seat against the window.

Levi nodded as the waitress poured him some coffee.

"Yes, he was quite an upstanding gentleman,"

Richard said.

"He certainly was. Poor chap had been ill for the last ten years, though. I'm surprised he held on as long as he did," said Nelson, who looked so much like Charles, they could have been brothers. He turned to Levi. "I attended the funeral but I don't remember seeing you there, Mr. Temple."

Levi thought fast. "Please call me Levi, and unfortunately, I was in France at the time of the funeral. I was looking to acquire some new art for Cornelius's collection."

"Ah, that man loved his art. Well, it was a nice funeral service. Too bad you missed it," Nelson said.

The waitress brought some croissants and took the men's orders. While there was a lull in the conversation, Levi looked around the dining room. He didn't see where Charles had disappeared to, but he soon noticed Penelope Juzan sitting in the corner. She was chatting with a man who had his back to Levi.

"Mr. Temple?" J.P. said.

"Oh, I'm sorry. Did you say something?" Levi said.

J.P. smiled. "I asked, how long did you know Cornelius?"

Levi sipped his coffee, trying not to look at Penny. "I've procured art for him for about five years now."

"Well, since he won't be using your services anymore, perhaps you could advise me on a few pieces. I'm sure my wife would love that."

"Certainly, Mr. Morgan. I'd be happy to."

"Please, call me J.P." He took a sip of his coffee.

"You could probably help us all," said Richard,

and the others nodded in agreement.

"It would be my pleasure." Levi sipped his coffee again and eyed Penny over the rim.

Nelson leaned over to him and said quietly, "Yes, that girl is a looker, but I'm sure she's not your type."

Levi looked at him, raising his eyebrows.

"She's not one of us, boy. She's got an air of...um, I don't know...street about her, if you know what I mean."

Levi moved his arms off the table so the waitress could place his omelet in front of him. "I thought she was somebody's niece or something."

Nelson nodded. "Yes, that's what I was told, too, though now I can't remember which family she's from. Anyways, she showed up here about a month ago, and she certainly likes to flirt with the men, but my wife mentioned she has worn the same dress to at least four events, so rumor has it she's not actually one of us and not quite as wealthy as she portrays. I'll tell you, my wife wouldn't be caught dead in the same dress twice." He chuckled as he cut into a thick slice of sugar ham. "That woman is only here looking for a rich husband."

Levi nodded. "I understand." He looked toward Penny again. "She is beautiful, though."

"That, she is, boy, that, she is, but I know those kinds of women. You take my word for it—she'll spend every penny you've got and more. She'll take your last dollar and leave you with absolutely nothing."

Levi laughed. "I'll keep that in mind, Nelson."

Charles returned after a few minutes and stood at the head of the table. He cleared his throat to get everyone's attention. "I have marvelous news, gentlemen. The staff has arranged for us to go quail hunting after breakfast, if you all would like to go."

They all nodded and acknowledge that they'd love to go.

Charles looked at Levi. "Mr. Temple, can you handle a gun? Would you like to join us?"

Levi once again looked across the room at Penny. Yes, she was beautiful, but he couldn't allow her to distract him from what he came here to do. He smiled at Charles.

"Yes, I'd love to accompany you."

Penelope Juzan

All through breakfast, Penny kept eyeing the table of gentlemen in the alcove. The young man from last night sat with his back against the windows and couldn't seem to take his eyes off her. "Do you see that young, blond gentleman over there by the windows?"

Her breakfast companion, George Turner, turned to see who she was talking about. "The man in the tie?"

"Yes. Do you know who he is?"

George stuffed a large slice of strawberry into his mouth. "No, I'm afraid I don't, but he's a little overdressed for breakfast, don't you think? Why are you interested in him?"

"No reason, really. I just saw him last night and wondered who he is."

Charles Lanier approached their table and clapped George on the back. "George, happy New Year to you." He nodded at Penny. "Miss Juzan."

She nodded and smiled back.

George placed his fork on the table and rose from the table. He pulled the napkin from his collar and wiped his hands on it before shaking Charles's hand. "Happy New Year to you, Charles."

"We're heading out to do some quail hunting this morning if you'd care to join us," Charles said.

"That sounds like a spectacular way to spend New Year's Day. What time are you going?"

"In a few minutes, as soon as everyone is ready. We're all going to change clothes and meet at the taxidermy shop downstairs. Would you care to come along?"

"Yes, I think I will. Thank you for asking."

When Charles left the table, George sat back down and Penny pouted. "What's the matter, dear?"

"I'd like to go, too, but I don't think those gentlemen would want a woman tagging along."

"Oh, nonsense, you can probably outshoot the whole lot of them. Why don't you run and change and we'll meet at the shop in a few minutes."

Penny rose and kissed George on the cheek. She was so excited to get out of these ruffled, scratchy clothes, she nearly skipped out of the dining room.

When she reached the dining room entrance, she glanced back at the table of men sitting by the window and saw the young, blond man still staring at her. She vowed to find out all about him before day's end.

Quail Hunting

On the first floor of the club there were a few shops: a beauty parlor, a tailor, and a hunting store that sold rifles and clothing, but none was busier than the taxidermy shop. In most social clubs, women carrying a gun and hunting was frowned upon, but the Jekyll Island Club was one of the only clubs in the country that encouraged women to hunt. Jekyll Island denizens would hunt daily for quail, duck, deer, pheasant, and the like, and the taxidermist would deliver the meat to the club's chef for the evening's supper and then the trophy to the hunter to decorate his or her mantel. Nearly every home on the island proudly displayed trophies in each and every room. Almost every evening, the Grand Dining Room had "Specials of the Day" that were freshly supplied by its members.

Levi ran back to the apartment to change into something a little less formal. He opted for his brown trousers and a brown shirt, and he topped the attire with a light tan hunting jacket. He admired himself in the mirror. "Yes, this will work nicely." He winked at his own reflection and grinned.

He walked back to the club, entered the taxidermy shop, and was taken aback by a large brown bear that stood in the entryway, teeth bared, poised for attack.

The taxidermist said from behind the counter, "Oh, don't worry about him. We don't have any bears on the island. He's just for show."

Levi looked at the taxidermist. "I wasn't worried. I've killed more dangerous things than a bear."

The man looked at Levi as if wondering what kind of animal would be more dangerous than a bear. Before he could ask, the men from the club entered the shop.

"Hi, Bernie," Nelson said to the taxidermist.

"Happy New Year, Bernie, old chap," J.P. chimed in.

Bernie smiled. "Good morning, gentlemen. How can I help you today?"

Charles closed the door behind him. "Bernie, we need some birdshot and..." He turned toward Levi. "Do you have a rifle, Levi?"

Levi shook his head.

"We need to borrow a gun for our new friend, Levi."

"Certainly," said Bernie, hustling behind the counter to dig out what Charles had requested. He held up a twelve-gauge shotgun. "Will this one do?"

"Levi, have you ever shot a gun before?" Charles asked.

Levi shrugged. "Yeah, a few times."

Charles turned back to Bernie. "Sure, that'll be fine."

Bernie placed the gun and some ammunition on the display case, which served as the sales counter. "Would you all like to go out by yourselves or would you like me to send a guide out with you?"

"We'd like guides, and how about some dogs? I hate plodding through the swamp, looking for the birds."

"All right. How many pairs will be going so I know how many dogs to send?"

"Let's see...me and Levi, J.P. and Nelson, John and Richard, and James and George." Charles turned again to Levi. "Levi, you didn't meet George Turner this morning, but he'll be joining us."

As if on cue, George Turner entered the small shop. Levi recognized him as the man Penny had been having breakfast with. Charles introduced them and they shook hands.

Charles turned to the shopkeeper and said, "There will be four pairs, Bernie."

The door opened again and Penny entered, looking as if she'd just emerged from the pages of *La Nouvelle Mode* fashion magazine. She wore a long brown topcoat that was flowing open, revealing a dark brown dress. On her head sat a small version of a black top hat. In her hands was a twelve-gauge shotgun. Levi had never seen a more scintillating sight in his life.

Apparently the other men thought the same, because they all stopped speaking and stared at her.

She froze near the doorway. Levi glanced around at the men and realized he was mistaken about why they were all suddenly silent. By the looks on their faces, he knew Penny was not welcome on this hunting trip, and he could tell by the look on her face that she was disappointed but not surprised.

"I'm sorry," she said. "George thought it would be all right if I tagged along."

Charles stepped forward. "Yes, of course, it's all right. We would love to have to join us, Miss Juzan. We have four pairs with guides and dogs, so you'll need to choose a pair to join." When James and John groaned behind him, and Nelson let out a loud sigh, Charles added, "You should join Levi and me."

Levi felt the hair on the back of his neck stand straight up. He would finally get to meet this elusive woman and spend the afternoon with her. Why, instead of eagerness, did he feel trepidation?

"Levi?" Charles looked back at him. "Will that be all right?"

Penny followed Charles's gaze and looked straight into Levi's eyes. Her green eyes were hypnotic, piercing straight into his soul.

"Um, sure, that'd be great," Levi stumbled.

"Good, then it's settled. Bernie, we'll meet you outside."

"Right away, Mr. Lanier."

The men single-filed out the door, passing Penny without much more than an obligatory nod. The last man left in the shop was Levi, who grabbed the gun off the counter, filled his pockets with ammunition, then turned and stared at her.

"Are you ready to go?" she asked politely.

"Um, yes." He began to walk past her, and then realized he should be a gentleman and let her go first. He stopped and gestured toward the door.

She smiled at him and exited the shop.

He followed and pulled the door closed behind him.

A Day on the Game Preserve

The wooden wagons, weathered and gray, pulled up almost immediately and everyone climbed aboard. The dogs barked from their crates in the back wagon, apparently as excited about the day's hunt as the hunters were. Levi climbed into the wagon behind the one Penny rode in, admiring her slim frame and her faux top hat. It was rare to see a woman these days without one of those big, floppy hats, and he liked it. He eyed the back of her neck, where her dark hair met ivory skin.

"Do you know how to handle that gun?" Charles asked in the tone of an overprotective father, interrupting Levi's carnal thoughts.

"Yes, sir, I'll manage it just fine."

"All right, then. You let me know if you need any help."

Levi nodded and looked back at Penny. Why was this woman so evocative to him?

When the group reached the game preserve on

the other side of the island, most of the men couldn't move fast enough to get away from the female who had joined them. As the dogs were removed from their crates, they seemed to mimic the men's enthusiasm, jumping and barking and pulling at their leashes. Each pair of men took two dogs and headed into the swampy fields. Soon, the only ones left in the clearing were Charles, Levi, and Penny.

Charles reached for the last two dogs, directing the guide to stay with the wagon. "I can handle the dogs."

Penny grinned at Charles and looked back at Levi. "You ready?"

Levi nodded.

They weren't more than a hundred yards from the wagons when they heard a horse gallop in their direction. "Mr. Lanier, Mr. Lanier," called the winded rider.

Charles stopped and turned around. "What is it, Ben?"

"They need you back at the club, sir. Something about the sheriff coming by."

Charles slumped and turned to Levi and Penny. "I'm afraid you kids will have to go on your own. That's what happens when you're the president of the club. Everything is an emergency you have to deal with."

"I'm so sorry, Mr. Lanier," Penny said. "Perhaps we can go hunting with you later in the week."

"That would be nice, Miss Juzan. I'll have the driver take me back and return to pick you up. Can you handle the dogs, Levi?"

Levi nodded.

Charles handed the dog's leashes to Levi and

plodded back to the wagon.

Levi shrugged at Penny, and they continued down the path toward the field, not a word between them. The dogs pulled against the leashes, sniffing each stone and every blade of grass.

After a few minutes, Penny broke the silence. "So, we haven't been properly introduced. My name is Penelope Juzan, but everyone calls me Penny."

Levi kept walking, his eyes on the path. The nearness of her made his hands sweat on the leashes and on his gun, which was propped up on his shoulder, muzzle pointing skyward. "It's very nice to meet you, Miss Juzan."

"Please call me Penny."

Levi nodded but didn't respond. He wondered if her kiss would elicit the same response in him that her smoky voice did. He glanced over at her full lips and assumed it would.

After another long silence, Penny asked, "So, what's your name?"

Levi startled as if awakened from a dream. "Oh, I'm sorry. My name is Levi. Levi Temple."

Penny stumbled on a thick patch of briar and almost landed on her face in the dirt, but Levi quickly grabbed her elbow, dropping both leashes in the process. Penny recovered but the dogs darted off into the brush. Levi and Penny watched as the dogs ran away.

"Are you all right?" Levi asked her.

Penny turned to him, her face a little pale. "Sure, I'm fine. I'm sorry. I don't know how I tripped on that briar." She looked back at the ground and up at Levi.

"What is it?" he asked, confused by the

expression in her eyes.

"Oh, it's nothing. Have we met before, Mr. Temple?"

"No, I'm sure I would have remembered someone as pretty as you." Levi gave her his dimpled grin. He had tried that smile on her last night on the beach but it didn't go over well.

She smiled back faintly and the slightest blush covered her cheeks.

He grinned even wider.

They turned and continued their walk. When they caught up with the dogs, they heard the crack of gunfire from over the small hill.

"Sounds like the others are already at work. We'd better get busy." Penny whistled for the dogs, who came right to her. She removed their leashes as Levi loaded his gun with birdshot. "Are you ready?" she asked.

He nodded.

She sent the dogs off into the brush, and not more than a few moments later, the blue sky was filled with a covey of quail taking flight. Levi and Penny simultaneously shot at them and each brought down a bird. They lowered their guns and looked at each other with a mixture of surprise and satisfaction.

"Nice shooting, Miss Juzan, er, Penny."

She beamed with pride. "And you, Levi."

The dogs scurried around until they found and brought both birds back and dropped them at Levi's and Penny's feet. Levi placed the birds in their hunting sack as Penny hooked the leashes back on the dogs.

As they continued their walk, Penny asked, "So, where are you from, Levi?"

"Oh, here and there. I grew up in the South, but

the last few years I've been on the East Coast, mostly in New York and New Jersey. How about you?"

"I'm actually from the South, too. I grew up in Vicksburg, Mississippi. Have you ever been there?"

"No, I'm afraid I haven't. What brings you to Georgia?"

"My uncle passed away and I felt bad I never came here with him, so I'm just visiting, sort of in his memory."

"I'm very sorry for your loss. Did he have a home here on the island?"

"Yes, he had an apartment in the annex, but I'm not staying at his apartment. In my aunt's grief, I didn't want to ask her for the key, so I'm staying in one of the suites."

"In the annex?"

"Yes."

"Oh, that's very nice. I'm staying in the annex also."

Before they could converse any further, they had arrived at a good hunting location and again set the dogs loose to scare up more quail. They felled two more birds. With their hunting bag full, they turned around and headed back to the wagon.

Their conversation seemed to falter as Penny stared at the ground and Levi looked off at the horizon, admiring the hills and flora of the beautiful island. When they reached the clearing, the guide locked the dogs in their crates and emptied the hunting bag onto the back of the wagon.

"Very nice birds you got here. Congratulations."

"Thank you," said Penny.

There was a commotion from their left as the other hunters returned from the expedition. J.P. and

Nelson were the first to emerge into the clearing.

Nelson admired the birds on the back of the wagon. "We had no luck at all. You two seemed to have done very well." He looked around. "Where's Charles?"

"He got called away on club business," Levi said, "so it was just Penny and me."

Nelson glanced at Penny with new admiration. "Well, Miss Juzan, you'll have to be my partner next time."

Penny smiled.

The final four hunters returned to the clearing shortly after, and the guide emptied their bags onto the wagon—a grand total of two birds. "Maybe you'll have better luck next time," the guide said. "We'll get these birds cleaned up right away."

"I can help you with that." Levi stepped forward, grabbed one of the birds by the neck, pulled out his pocketknife, and cut the bird open, beak to tail.

The other men froze and stared at him.

"What?" Levi said, looking from one face to the next.

"We don't do that sort of thing, Levi," Nelson said. "The taxidermist will take care of it."

"Oh." Levi stood motionless, blood dripping from the bird into a big puddle at his feet. "I'm sorry. I'm used to fending for myself while in the wilderness."

The men didn't move.

"Please forgive me." He handed the bloody bird to the guide.

The guide handed Levi a cloth to wipe his hands on, and the group boarded the wagons and headed back to the club.

Levi sat next to Penny in the wagon, so close to her he could feel the heat from her thigh through her dress. He leaned toward her and could smell the soap and perfume on her skin. "Well, that was embarrassing," he whispered into her ear.

"Don't worry about it," she whispered back. "They need a little blood to shake them up every once in a while." She smiled at him, only a couple inches from his face, her green eyes glistening with mischief.

He pulled out his silver lighter and flipped it open and closed.

"What's that you have there?"

He held it up for her to see. "It's a lighter."

"Oh, it looks like fish scales. It's very attractive. Do you smoke, Mr. Temple?"

"No, I don't. I just like the weight of it in my hands. It's just a trinket."

After a few minutes of silence between them, Levi asked, "Would you like to have supper with me this evening, Miss Juzan?"

"I'm sorry, but I have a prior supper engagement. Maybe another time."

She looked away and remained silent for the rest of the journey.

The Grand Dining Room

When Levi arrived in the Grand Dining Room that evening, he looked around at the elegant women in flamboyant hats and the gentlemen in handsome suits, searching for a familiar face to dine with. He spotted Nelson at a table in the corner with his wife and family. Levi remained for a moment in the doorway, and fortunately, Nelson spotted him and waved him over. Nelson's family smiled at Levi as he approached.

Nelson stood up and shook his hand. "Levi, I'd like you to meet my wife, Abigail; my daughter, Abby; her husband, John; and our grandsons—little John, little Nelson, and baby Lawrence."

Levi nodded at the ladies and shook John's hand.

"Oh, my father mentioned you today, Levi. He said you're quite a good shot on the game preserve," John said.

"I'm sorry, I don't know who your father is."

"I'm John Rockefeller's son."

"Oh, you're John Jr., so this young man must be John the third." Levi gestured toward the eldest of the three boys.

"Yes, that's right." John said.

"We just ordered," said Nelson, gesturing toward the table. "Would you care to join us for supper?"

"Yes, I'd love to. Thank you."

Nelson nodded toward the maître d', who immediately brought another chair to the already crowded table.

John turned to his wife. "Abby, are you feeling all right, dear? You don't look so well."

She shook her head. "I don't really feel all that well. Probably just a little tired. Would you all mind if I skipped dinner and returned to the house?"

"Not at all, dear," John said. "Would you like me to accompany you?"

Nelson's wife spoke up. "I'll go with her, John. You men stay and enjoy your supper. I'll take Abby and the boys back to the house." She turned to her husband. "Nelson, will you please ask the waiter to package our dinners and deliver them to the house?"

"Of course, my dear."

The men rose as the ladies did. Nelson kissed his wife and daughter and ruffled his grandsons' hair.

"Good night, Grandpa," the boys said. "Goodnight, Papa."

"I'll see you all in the morning," John said to his boys.

When Abby stood, Levi noticed she was pregnant. He assumed with three boys under the age of four and another on the way, she must've been extremely tired. *I'd go back to my room, too.*

After the women and children left, John resumed his discussion about Levi's fine shooting abilities.

"So where did you learn to shoot, Levi?"

"I grew up in Mississippi. It's a way of life there. I think most boys there can shoot before they can walk."

They all laughed.

"Certainly different than where I grew up. I was groomed from a very young age to take over my father's business. We weren't allowed the luxury of being outdoors very often. We were always in school."

Levi thought he should redeem himself and not appear to be a country hick. "Well, I attended school also."

"Really? Where did you go?"

"I went to Brown."

"Really? Me, too! What year did you graduate?"

"I graduated in 1909. Haven't really decided what I want to do with my life yet." Levi smiled, knowing full well that the man sitting across from him had gone to Brown, graduated in 1897, and was a member of Alpha Delta Phi.

"That's great! I graduated in 1897. Guess I'm a bit older than you, huh?"

"Just a little bit," Levi teased.

When the waiter brought bread and butter to the table, Nelson took the opportunity to break into the conversation. "So, Levi, you got to spend the day with the beautiful Penelope Juzan. Is she everything you dreamed?"

A huge grin formed on Levi's face. "Yes, I did, and not only is she beautiful, she's also charming and intelligent. And a great shot."

"I told you about that woman. Don't say I didn't warn you when she leaves you penniless. Penny-less, get it?" He laughed at his own joke.

Levi laughed as he buttered a slice of bread and took a huge bite. He hadn't eaten since breakfast and was starving.

"Wait, who's Penelope Juzan?" John asked.

"That brunette with the big green eyes who flirts with all the men," Nelson said.

"Oh, that's Cornelius's niece," said John.

Levi choked on his piece of bread.

"Whoa, there. Are you all right, son?" Nelson patted him on the back.

Levi grabbed his glass of water and took a drink to wash down the bread. "Yes, I'm fine."

"So, if Miss Juzan is Cornelius's niece, I'd think you would already know her, Levi," Nelson said.

Levi composed himself. "Well, I certainly don't know all of Cornelius's family, and Penny told me she lived in Vicksburg. I've never been there."

"You ever heard Cornelius mention family in Vicksburg?" Nelson asked.

Levi shook his head. "Nope, I'm afraid not."

Levi scanned the room for Penny. She'd told him she had a supper date but he didn't see her there. That was probably a good thing. He needed time to think about this revelation of Cornelius being her uncle.

After supper, Levi went for a walk down the beach, taking advantage of the time to think through every angle he could use to counter anyone who might claim he wasn't Cornelius's business partner. He decided he would have to locate Penny and find out exactly how close she and her deceased uncle were.

When he arrived at his apartment a few hours

later, there was a piece of paper taped to the door.

Dear Mr. Levi Temple,

We request the honor of your presence
at our annual event
The January Social.
Saturday the sixth of January
Nineteen hundred twelve.
Solterra Cottage
Lot 28 (north of the clubhouse)
Dining and cocktails at 6:00 in the evening
Attire is casual

Sincerely,
Frederic and Emma Baker

The January Social

Levi spent the next few days searching for Penny but she was nowhere to be found. In the meantime, he met a few more of the island's winter residents and found himself at ease in their circle. He spent his days playing bridge and billiards and was even invited to visit the Hamptons for the summer, which he happily accepted. He was relishing every moment.

On the evening of January 6, he strolled down the sandy lane past the club, heading toward the January Social at Solterra Cottage. When he rounded the corner, the sight of the mansion was absolutely stunning. "Why do these people refer to these enormous homes as cottages?" he whispered to himself, then looked around to make sure no one was within earshot.

This was the largest private home he had ever seen, almost as big as the annex, which was as large as the clubhouse. The "cottage" was a handsome three-story structure, built in a Queen Anne style, with white walls and a steep roof, covered with cypress shingles. Turrets rose from the third floor, and there was even a gazebo at the end of the covered wraparound porch. Warm golden light cascaded from every window. The house was surrounded by azaleas, hyacinths, ferns, and palms, and he imagined the blooming flowers in the spring would make it look even more magnificent.

Laughter came from the back of the house so Levi followed the sound. When he reached the wrought-iron gate and opened it, he came face to face with Penny. She was wearing a dark purple velvet gown and looked stunning.

"Hello, Miss Juzan. I haven't seen you for a few days."

"Good evening, Levi. I didn't realize you'd be here tonight."

"Well, I got an invitation." He waved the piece of paper.

"That's nice. Listen, I have to run. I promised someone I'd be right back to continue a discussion. Have a nice evening."

She turned away and he yelled after her, "All right, I'll talk to you later," but she was already gone.

He closed the gate and entered the garden. Through the wisteria-covered arbor, he could see a well-manicured yard full of people chatting and socializing. He nodded and smiled at the people nearest the arbor and looked around for a familiar face. He found Charles on the cobblestone patio sitting with the senior John Rockefeller.

"Good evening, gentlemen," Levi said as he sprang up the two patio steps.

Charles looked up and smiled. "Oh, good evening, Levi." He rose to shake Levi's hand. "I hear you and Penny shot some fine birds."

Levi nodded. "Yes, indeed. That lady is a pretty good shot." He turned to John Sr. and extended his hand. "And, I met your son in the Grand Dining Room the other night. Nice lad."

"Yes, he's a good man. He makes my life a lot easier."

"Why don't you have a seat and join us?" Charles said.

Levi sat on one of the wrought-iron chairs. He enjoyed the feeling of sinking down into the flowered cushion. "So, John, your son works with you?"

"Yes, he's a lifesaver. My business has grown so large, I don't know what I'd do without him. Do you work for your father, Levi?"

Levi shook his head. "No, I'm afraid my father never cared for art and that's where my heart lies, so we followed our own paths."

"Is your father still living?"

"No, sir, he died a few years back."

"Oh, I'm sorry to hear that. Well, it looks like he left you well off."

"Yes, sir, he certainly did."

Charles rose from his chair. "Well, I'm going to find the missus and go inside to get a bite to eat."

"That's a good idea," John rose and followed Charles through the double doors.

Levi followed them into the enormous house, and just as he suspected, it was elegantly furnished. He was immediately convinced the Waldorf-Astoria would have nothing on this place. The furniture was massive and sophisticated. He entered the walnut-paneled dining room and found a dozen people sitting around a huge dining table, with room for more. The table could probably hold twenty people and probably belonged in a castle somewhere in Ireland rather than off a sandy road on Jekyll Island. Levi wondered how much a table like that would cost and how in the world anyone would move it onto an island. Another dozen guests lingered at the buffet stations set up along the walls. Roast beef, lobster, filet—it was a banquet fit for a king and the aromas were intoxicating. Levi hadn't realized how hungry he was.

After he filled his plate with lobster and roasted venison, he looked around for Charles and John but didn't see them anywhere. He wandered into the living room to see if they had ventured there. The living room was also large, with floor-to-ceiling windows overlooking the covered porch. Plush sofas and chairs in shimmering fabrics rested on expensive rugs that covered most of the parquet floor. The far wall was a floor-to-ceiling, fieldstone fireplace with a buck's head mounted in the middle. In front of the fireplace stood Penny surrounded by three men. Levi was positive one was the cad he'd seen her with in the billiard room at the club on New Year's Eve. He willed himself to not grimace at the man, and he sat down opposite the fireplace so he could watch Penny while he ate. She kept making eye contact with him, but he couldn't tell if she was interested in him or if she was wondering why he was staring at her. The woman was definitely hard to read.

Throughout the evening, he made sure he ended up wherever she was, keeping an eye out for an opportunity to speak with her about her uncle. The opportunity never presented itself. No matter where she was, she was always surrounded by suitors. Apparently, Levi wasn't the only man on the island who found her attractive.

Around midnight, after fostering his courage with a few drinks, he approached her and her entourage.

"Good evening, gentlemen. Penny." He nodded at them.

"Hello, Levi. Have you met these fine gentlemen yet?"

"No, I'm afraid I haven't."

Penny made the introductions—Frank, Samuel, and Horace. Levi shook hands with each of them. They seemed harmless enough.

"So, where are you from, Levi?" Frank asked.

"I travel between New York and New Jersey. I've been looking for a place to settle down in, but nothing has caught my eye yet."

"When are *you* going to settle down, Penny?" Samuel asked.

Penny shrugged. "Since my uncle passed away, I'm not really sure what to do next."

Samuel looked at Levi. "Her uncle died back in October." He looked back at Penny. "Cornelius was a good man. He's greatly missed by all of us."

Levi sipped his drink and didn't say anything for a moment, then he figured he might as well get it out in the open. "I worked with Mr. Bliss for the last couple years, procuring art for his collection."

Penny looked at him strangely but didn't say anything. Levi didn't know what he saw in her eyes. Was it confusion? It looked like fear, but fear of what? He felt an uncomfortable tingle on the back of his neck. He was the one who should be afraid, not her. Being Bliss's niece, she could easily destroy his entire plan.

"Did you two meet through her uncle?" Samuel

asked Levi.

Levi shook his head. "No, I'm afraid Cornelius never introduced us."

"I wonder why that is?" Penny asked, but it sounded more like a statement than a question. Levi stared at her and felt like he was drowning in her eyes.

He reluctantly turned his attention back to the men and continued conversing with them while occasionally glancing at Penny. They spoke of art and travel and the beautiful home they were standing in. The January Social was an annual event hosted by Frederic and Emma Baker. Mr. Baker had served as a club officer for nearly twenty years and knew everyone on the island. He was currently serving as the third vice president, which was more an honorary title than a position that required any actual work, but since he was in his eighties, that was probably a good thing. The men said Mr. Baker was a New York banker with a home on Fifth Avenue, a summer house in the Hamptons, and this winter house. Samuel said the Bakers had more money than God. Levi wondered how much money that was.

Penny seemed to perk up during this part of the conversation. Her face changed from whatever emotion Levi witnessed before to blatant excitement. "So, Levi, tell us—how did you come into your fortune?"

"It just fell into my lap." Levi chuckled and the other men followed suit, albeit uncomfortably.

"What? Did you find an old trunk full of gold or something?" She giggled and took a sip of her champagne, staring at Levi over the rim.

Levi looked her square in the eyes and smirked. "Yes, that's exactly what happened."

The other men laughed again while Penny and

Levi stared at each other. He was almost certain he could entice her into spending more time with him.

As night fell and the guests said their good-byes, Levi offered to walk Penny back to the annex. She reluctantly agreed and took his arm.

During their walk, she said, "So, tell me the truth, Levi. Where did you come into your fortune?"

Levi shuffled across the sand-covered lane, looking off toward the ocean, listening to the distant waves pounding the shore. "My father died and left everything to me. It was that simple."

"Did you say you were originally from the South?"

"Yes, ma'am. Lauderdale County, Mississippi."

Penny didn't say anything else as they continued their walk. When they reached her second-floor suite in the annex, she curtly wished him a good night and left him standing in the hallway. He took the stairs down to his apartment, lit the fireplace, and stared into the flames for a long time, thinking about how fascinating Penny was. She was indeed a lovely woman, but something in his gut told him she was going to be trouble. He had the same feeling one might have just as he's about to jump into deep water, not knowing what lies below the surface. It made Levi both exhilarated and apprehensive. With all of her questions about his money, he wondered if Nelson's warnings were indeed accurate. Maybe she was just looking for a rich husband. Levi smiled at the thought.

Perhaps he could be that man.

A Surprise Visitor

Penny closed the front door of her suite and turned the lock. She heard someone behind her, and her heart raced with alarm as she spun around. Someone grabbed her and put a hand over her mouth. She looked up into the black eyes of a Choctaw Indian.

"Shhh," he said as he slowly removed his hand. "It's me."

"Luke!" she whispered, hoping Levi wasn't still on the other side of the door. She wrenched herself out of his grasp. "What are you doing here?"

"I came to check on you."

"I don't need a babysitter. You shouldn't be here."

"I think you do need a babysitter. I saw you from the window. Who was that man you were walking with?"

"That's none of your business." She stormed past him, removing her velvet wrap and tossing it across the back of the dining room chair on her way to the kitchen.

He followed her, watched her light the stove and place a teakettle on top.

She and Luke had grown up together and were just like brother and sister. They were both eleven years old when her father, Theodore Juzan, was found collapsed at his desk. Not only had he had been her world, he was also the only father Luke had ever known, and Luke cried for days on end after his death. The void her father left was still felt deeply by both over ten years later.

After her father died in 1901, Penny and her mother slowly returned to their way of life. They remained on the plantation with Luke overseeing the farm and his mother, Ina, running the household.

In 1905, catastrophe struck again when Luke's mother was found crumpled in the field. She had been traversing to her cottage from the main plantation house. One of the workers ran into the main house, screaming that Miss Ina had done died. Penny would never forget that day or the pained look on Luke's face.

Following Ina's death, Penny's mother begged Luke to move from the cottage into the main house but Luke refused. He wanted to remain in his mother's cottage on the back of the property. He dealt with the loss by spending long days working the soil, tending the animals, and running the plantation's business. Penny didn't see much of him for the next few years besides the occasional sighting of him on horseback or at the far end of a field, overseeing the farmhands.

In early 1910, Penny's mother became bedridden with pneumonia and Luke stayed in the main house to help Penny take care of her. She only suffered from her illness a few short days before it claimed her life. After the funeral, Penny asked Luke to stay in the main house with her. He knew her father would've expected that of him so he obliged. The two were nearly inseparable for a year after that. They worked all day on the plantation and spent the evenings together on the front porch, watching the sun set over the mighty Mississippi. They drank tea and fanned themselves, futilely trying to ward off the oppressive Mississippi humidity. Life was mundane, boring, even.

One afternoon, Penny was in the attic sorting through her parents' belonging, looking for items to donate to the local church fundraiser, and she came across her great grandfather's old journals. They were leather bound and covered in nearly an inch of dust. They obviously hadn't been touched in many years. Penny thumbed through them and found them written by her great grandfather, Pierre Juzan. They were filled with names of guests who stayed at his inn, accounting documents from the running of the tavern and farm, and inventory lists of what was purchased and sold.

When she reached the middle of the last journal, the multiple topics narrowed to one—a trunk of gold. Penny read the story of Pierre and Leon—Luke's great-grandfather—and their quest for the trunk. In August of 1841, the journal ended. Penny remembered her father telling her both Pierre and Leon died in 1841. She assumed that was the reason for the abrupt ending of journal entries, and she wondered what had happened to the gold the two had so desperately tried to get their hands on. She flipped a few more pages and found more entries, but this time they were dated 1900 and 1901 and were written in her father's hand. They told of the discovery of the trunk at the bottom of Lake Juzan, and the final entry was a piece of paper stuck between the pages of the old book. It was a letter from a man named Carter Stuckey, saying he had retrieved the trunk from Lake Juzan and was on his way back to Vicksburg. Penny remembered Carter Stuckey. He was the elderly white-haired man who used to oversee their plantation. She sat on the floor of the attic trying to remember if she had seen Carter Stuckey after her father's death. She didn't think so, and she assumed he and the trunk had never arrived.

A few months later, she travelled to Lake Juzan and spoke with the sheriff of Lauderdale County. His name was J.R. Temple. He told her Carter Stuckey had been murdered out at Stuckey's Inn by Thomas Stuckey. She didn't tell him about the missing gold, but she knew a heavy trunk of gold just wouldn't up and walk away. She pried information out of the sheriff that someone else was around at the time of Carter Stuckey's death—someone who may have answers—or possibly may have the gold itself. She set her sights on finding that someone, and against Luke's wishes, she sold off every bit of her father's plantation to finance her quest.

Now a year later, she didn't want to rehash all of this with Luke. She turned to him and placed her hands on her hips. "So, really, what are you doing here?"

"I just wanted to make sure you were all right. I haven't heard from you in over a month. Have you found anything yet?"

She shrugged her shoulders. "I'm not sure. Maybe."

He plopped down on the tall chair next to the kitchen counter. "What do you mean, maybe?"

She looked at him. "Well..."

"Oh, my good lord, you found him, didn't you?"

"I think so." She could barely contain her excitement.

"Well, tell me everything."

She pulled two teacups from the cupboard and held one toward Luke, but he shook his head. "His name is Levi Temple."

Luke's mouth opened and then closed again. After a few moments, he laughed and said, "You're not serious."

She grinned at him. "Yes, I am serious, so you need to get out of here before you ruin everything." She poured herself a cup of tea and carried it past Luke into the living room.

He followed her and sat in the chair adjacent to the sofa, where she was sitting. "Penny, listen to me. You're playing a dangerous game here. You're going to get yourself killed doing this, or worse, you'll get everything you're after and bring the curse down on yourself."

"Luke, there is no curse. It's just misfortune or bad luck, that's all."

"And what makes you think you won't be the next victim of the same misfortune?"

"Because it's mine, that's why." She glared at him, and then looked into her teacup, clenching her teeth, aggravated that he was questioning her.

"It was your great grandfather's, too, and look what happened to him."

She exhaled and rolled her eyes.

After watching her in silence for a moment, Luke said, "Why would he call himself Levi Temple?"

"Well, why not?" she answered, her body

relaxing. "He couldn't go around calling himself Levi Stuckey. There's got to be somebody looking for a man by that name, isn't there? Sheriff Temple told me when Levi Stuckey was a twelve-year-old boy who disappeared ten years ago. He was slim and had dark blond hair. Levi Temple is about twenty-two. He fits the age and description perfectly. He would need to change his name in case they were still looking for him, and I probably wouldn't even think it was him except for the name."

"That all happened a decade ago, Penny. Surely no one would be looking for him now. They would probably assume he was dead or long gone." Luke shook his head and rubbed his chin. "Are you sure it's him?"

"Yes, I'm positive."

"How can you tell?"

"No one else notices, but he doesn't fit in here. He dresses just a little differently. He says things and does things that are just a little inappropriate. Something about him is a bit off, but I don't think it's blatant enough for anyone else to pick up on. I notice because I've been watching him like a hawk."

Luke got up and stacked some logs in the fireplace. "I'd be happy to get out of your way and let you continue your search, but I really need to stay and rest for a few days. I hitched a ride all the way to Birmingham, where I hopped a train, then I had to sneak aboard a boat from the mainland to the island. It was a long trip and I haven't slept for days. I'm exhausted. I'll agree to stay out of sight if you'll bring me some supper from that fancy clubhouse."

"All right, deal, but you have to stay in the apartment. Your Indian features will stick out like a sore thumb around here."

"Yeah, I know." He stood close to the growing fire, warming himself. "So, do you have a plan?"

"Not yet. There's a slight problem with my cover."

"Yeah? What's that?"

"Levi is telling everyone he's the business partner of Cornelius Bliss. I told everyone Mr. Bliss was my poor deceased uncle."

"Well, if his relationship with Mr. Bliss is a lie like yours, he won't question you or say anything to anyone. He wouldn't want to blow his own cover by rocking the boat."

"Yeah, you're probably right," Penny said quietly as she stared into the flames.

Luke looked around the apartment. "So, is there more than one bedroom here, or shall I sleep with you?" He smiled.

"You can sleep on the couch," she said.

Break Down

With the morning sunlight on his face, Levi was walking across the dewy grass on his way to breakfast when he heard Nelson's voice.

"A Break Down is to end a turn by making a mistake," Nelson said.

Something about the definition made Levi laugh. *A breakdown would be a mistake in itself*, he thought.

He walked toward the sound of Nelson's voice and found him explaining the rules of croquet to none other than Penny Juzan.

"Good morning, you two. Are you going to play a game this morning?"

"Good morning, Levi. I was just explaining the rules to Penny. We were planning on a game after breakfast. Would you care to play with us?"

Levi smiled at Penny. "Yes, of course, I'd love to. You'll have to refresh my memory on the rules also. It's been a long time since I played a serious game of croquet."

"How long has it been, Levi?" Penny asked. Her face held a slight grin, almost as if she was taunting him.

Levi assumed she would be as good at croquet as she was at shooting. "It's been a very long time, but I'll do my best."

"Why don't you kids run along and get a table for breakfast, and I'll track down my wife and join you, then we'll play a foursome."

"Sounds good, Nelson." Levi offered his arm to Penny.

She reluctantly took it and together they climbed the steps of the club.

By the time the maître d' led them to a table, Nelson and his wife, Abigail, had arrived. The four sat down together.

Throughout the meal, Levi made small talk with Penny, but he couldn't seem to get her attention. Her eyes kept darting around the room as if she were looking for something or expecting to see someone. The conversation remained between Levi and Nelson, with them discussing hunting and Abigail politely nodding on occasion. Between Abigail's silence, Penny's distraction, and the men chatting about hunting, the four enjoyed a breakfast of pancakes covered with thick maple syrup shipped down from Michigan.

The moment they finished eating, Penny threw down her napkin, jumped up from the table, and excused herself. Levi watched her walk away, wondering where she was going. He also wondered if he would ever be able to reach her. Sometimes she seemed to warm up to him, and the next minute, she was as cold as a snake. Nelson watched Levi's face as

Penny disappeared through the doorway.

"What's wrong, son? Can't get the girl to notice you?" Nelson laughed.

"I'm working on it. Give me some time." Levi smiled at the teasing.

"Well, you remember what I said about that girl."

"Yes, sir." Levi nodded.

Abigail placed her napkin on the table.

"Are you ready to go, my dear?"

Abigail nodded.

"Let's start our game, then." Nelson pulled out his wife's chair and helped her to her feet. He then told the waiter to escort Penny out to the front lawn when she returned.

The men and Abigail were choosing their colors in preparation for their game when Penny approached them. "I'm sorry. I had to take care of something. Are we partners or do we play on our own?"

"Whatever you'd like to do, Penny," Nelson said.

Penny looked at Levi with that spark of competitiveness in her eyes. "I think I'd like to play on my own."

The game was a close match between Nelson and Penny, with Abigail and Levi trailing miserably behind, but in the end, Nelson allowed Penny to win. He lost the game by missing a swing, what is called a Break Down. Levi was certain Penny didn't like winning by default, but she remained a gracious champion.

After Nelson and Abigail bid their good-byes, Levi asked Penny if she would like to go on a carriage ride.

"Thank you very much for the offer, but I'm afraid I have things I need to take care of today. Maybe some other time." She smiled and walked away, leaving Levi alone on the lawn, surrounded by mallets and wickets.

"What is going on with that woman?" Levi mumbled to himself as he watched her stroll back into the club. He planted himself on a bench between some willow trees and waited for her. When she emerged again, he watched her descend the club steps, carrying a white sack used for packaging meals. He wondered why she would take food home when they had just finished breakfast. He knew one thing for sure—this woman was going to drive him to drink. He returned to the club and requested a bottle of whiskey.

He spent the rest of the day in his apartment, sipping out of the bottle. It had been a long time since he'd had a real drink instead of one of those fruity cocktails they served around this place, and he relished the flavor of the strong, brown liquid as he swished it around his mouth. Sparkling champagne and imported wine just weren't his flavor. He took sip after sip, sitting in front of the picture window and watching the world go by. He didn't realize how much he had drunk until the sun began to set and he rose to go get some supper.

He hadn't stumbled more than a few yards down the path toward the club when a young girl in a white apron approached him and asked if he was all right.

"I'm fine. Just a little tipsy, that's all."

"Can I help you back to your room, sir?"

"I was going to the dining room for supper."

"Oh, sir, they wouldn't like to see you there in this condition. How about I walk you back to your room and bring you some supper? Would that be all right?"

Levi tipped his head back and looked at her down the bridge of his nose. "You're quite pretty."

"Thank you, sir," she said as she took his arm, spun him around, and led him back toward the annex. "Which room are you staying in, sir?"

"Apartment two. Would you like to have supper with me? I'm sorry I don't know your name."

"My name is Fanny, sir."

"Well, Fanny, would you do me the honor of having supper with me?"

Fanny blushed. "Well, I just finished my shift and I'm starving, so I would like that very much."

Another

The next morning on her way to breakfast, Penny overheard a couple of the waitresses talking behind the club. Another servant girl had been found strangled at daybreak. The girl's name was Fanny and she was a waitress at the club, but she hadn't shown up for work this morning. The last time anyone saw her was when she came into the kitchen late last night and ordered two meals packaged. She told the cook she would deliver them herself but didn't say to whom.

As Penny ate breakfast, she watched the sheriff and his deputy wandering through the club, asking questions of the guests. She knew they had kept the New Year's Eve incident out of the papers, but she didn't know if they would be able to do the same with a second death.

Nelson approached her. "Penny, have you heard what happened?"

"Yes, Nelson, it's tragic. Who would do such a thing?"

"I don't know, my dear, but I would implore you to always keep an escort with you until we find out who did this. I don't think any of you ladies are safe right now. As a matter of fact, I'm going to speak with Charles about implementing some security around here."

"That's a good idea, and I'll make sure I always have someone with me, especially at night."

Nelson nodded and left Penny alone to finish her breakfast. As she sipped her tea, she listened in on the conversation between two men at the table next to hers.

"Of course they were murdered. Do you think they strangled themselves?"

"No, of course not, but who would do such a thing? This island has been the safest place on earth since it opened, and we know every single member here. We even know all their servants."

"Maybe it's someone new. Who has just recently arrived?"

After a moment of silence, the second man spoke. "Well, there are only a couple people I can think of—Mr. Temple and Miss Juzan."

"From what I hear, they were both related to Cornelius Bliss. I can't believe either of them would have anything to do with those girls getting killed, but I guess one never knows."

Penny jumped up from her chair and sprinted from the dining room. She lifted her long skirt with one hand and held her hat on her head with the other, and she ran as fast as she could across the yard and up the sandy road. By the time she reached her suite, she was covered in sweat.

"My goodness, Penny, what is it?" Luke asked.

"A servant girl was murdered last night," she said while panting, trying to catch her breath. She leaned her back against the closed door.

"Murdered? Here?"

Penny nodded. "That's the second one. Another servant girl was killed on New Year's Eve."

"You didn't tell me that. That's it. I can't have you in danger. You're packing this very minute and coming home with me." Luke reached for her hand, with deep concern etched across his face.

"No!" she shouted and pulled away from his touch. "No, I'm not leaving. I've come too far to stop now."

Luke dropped his arm and shook his head. "Penny, if people are being murdered on this island, this is no place for you. The money isn't worth your life."

"I don't have anything to go back to, Luke. I sold everything I owned to be here. I don't have a choice. I must stay and see this through." She dropped her head into her hands and began to cry.

"Why are you crying? Did you know either of the girls?"

"No, I'm not crying for them. I'm crying for me."

Luke remained silent.

After a moment, she wiped the tears from her face, took a deep breath, and straightened her shoulders. "I overheard two men in the dining room say the murderer must be one of the newcomers to the island, and the only newcomers are me and Levi."

Luke's eyes widened. "Someone would think you had something to do with this? That's unbelievable."

Penny nodded. She headed toward the kitchen and Luke trailed behind her.

"Penny, if you didn't do it, and they've narrowed it down to you or Levi, then..."

Penny gasped and spun around, her hand at her mouth. "I didn't think of that. Levi is a killer?"

"Well, you don't know that, but what if he is?"

Penny didn't answer him. She turned and looked out the front window. Luke remained quiet for a few minutes but he finally spoke up.

"Penny, if Levi is a killer, I don't want you anywhere near that man. I want you to stay far away from him."

Penny continued staring at the window as she spoke in a low, controlled tone. "No, Luke. I need to get close to him. But if Levi is a killer, I need to be armed." She looked at him. "Can you get me a pistol?"

Luke sighed and nodded. He walked into the bedroom and returned carrying a Colt six-shooter, which he handed to Penny. "We should go out to the game preserve and I'll teach you how to use it."

She reached for the pistol. "I already know how to use it."

Cat and Mouse

Over the next week, the sheriff and his deputies interviewed everyone on the island, and the sheriff came to the same conclusion as the two men talking at breakfast the morning the second body was discovered. Everyone on the island had known each other for years. Nothing remotely illegal or dangerous had ever happened there. Not until there were newcomers, and the only newcomers to the island were Penny and Levi.

The sheriff met with Levi and found that he had been seen by dozens of people the entire evening of New Year's Eve. During the second murder, he said he'd been drunk in his apartment—alone. No one heard him from the adjacent apartments, but the sheriff spoke with the tenant upstairs who said there was music playing in Levi's apartment all evening. The tenant had been so agitated by the noise, he was tempted to go downstairs and request Levi turn the music off, but he said Levi must have gone to bed by eleven because the sound quieted about that time.

The only person the sheriff had left to interview was Penelope Juzan. He knocked on her door and she immediately answered.

"Oh, hello, Sheriff. What can I do for you?"

"Good morning, Miss Juzan. May I come in and speak with you for a minute?"

"Certainly, Sheriff. Come on in." She stepped back to allow the sheriff into the suite. "Would you care for something cool to drink?"

The sheriff shook his head as he removed his hat and held it by the brim, spinning it around every few seconds. "Miss Juzan, I'd like to know what you know about the two girls who were murdered."

"I'm afraid I don't know anything, Sheriff. I saw the first girl on the beach the same time as everyone else. I didn't find out about the second girl until I was having breakfast in the dining room that morning."

"Can you tell me where you were on New Year's Eve?"

"Sure, I was at the party at the club. When the girl's body was discovered on the beach, I was on the patio with Mr. Goodyear."

"I've spoken with everyone about that night. Mr. Goodyear didn't mention being with you that evening."

Penny blushed. "Well, he was pretty intoxicated. I wouldn't be surprised if he didn't remember trying to kiss me on the patio. That's when we heard the woman screaming on the beach and we all ran down there."

"Kiss you, huh? Well, where were you the evening of last Sunday, the seventh?"

"I was here in my suite. I didn't go out all evening."

"Were you alone all evening?"

"Why, yes, I was." She looked surprised. "I don't understand what you're asking, Sheriff."

"I was hoping you might have had a visitor, you know, someone who could corroborate your story."

"Why would I need that? I didn't murder those girls. I never even heard of them until they showed up dead."

The sheriff turned toward the door. "Well, Miss Juzan, I'm going to speak with Mr. Goodyear again and see if he remembers being with you on New Year's Eve."

* * *

Penny stood mute as she watched the sheriff leave her suite and close the door. She stared at the wooden door in disbelief that he would actually consider her a suspect.

Luke emerged from the bedroom. "You should have told him you were with me last Sunday night."

"Luke, no one can know you're here. They'll really suspect something if they think I'm carrying on with an Indian." Penny put the side of her thumb up to her lips and chewed on her nail.

"Well, it's obvious they suspect you in these murders."

"I know, I know. Shhhh. Let me think." She went down the hall into the bedroom and closed the door behind her, leaving Luke alone in the living room.

Later that evening, a second knock came on the door. Penny shooed Luke from the room and opened the door, expecting the sheriff again, but she came face to face with Levi. He leaned his shoulder on the doorjamb and grinned at her.

"Hello, Penny."

"Um, hello, Levi. Can I help you?"

"I certainly hope so. I was wondering if you would like to have supper with me this evening. It's a lovely, warm night, and I thought it'd be nice to have candlelight supper and take a stroll on the beach."

"Well, I don't know..."

"Come on. It's a full moon and there's not a cloud in the sky."

She sighed.

"It'll be lovely, I promise."

"Oh, all right. Hang on and let me get my wrap." Penny didn't invite him in and closed the door in his face. She returned with a purple shawl in one hand, a large brimmed hat covered in silk flowers in the other hand, and a clutch purse tucked under her arm. She pulled the door closed and tried to wrap the shawl around her shoulders, but fumbled with her purse and hat.

"May I hold those for you?" Levi offered.

"No!" Penny snapped. "I'm sorry, I mean, I've got it all under control. Thank you anyways."

Levi shrugged and waited for her to place the wrap on her shoulders and the hat on her head. When she was finally situated, he offered his arm to escort her to the club.

After they were seated and had ordered a bottle of wine, Penny said, "The sheriff questioned me about the murdered girls this morning."

"He did? I think he's questioning everyone." Levi sipped his wine and tore a piece of bread from the loaf in the basket on the table.

"He seemed worried that I didn't have an alibi for last Sunday night, and also that the man I was with on the patio when the girl was found on New Year's Eve didn't mention being with me." She tore a piece of bread from the loaf and was sliding the butter knife over it when she stopped and looked at Levi. "Wait a minute! You were on the patio that night, too! You saw me there, didn't you?"

Levi swallowed his bread and chased it with a drink of wine. "Yes, I think I remember seeing you on the patio." He gave her a dimpled grin.

"Will you tell the sheriff that you were with me?"

"Well, I wasn't exactly *with* you, but I'll mention it to him if you think it'll help."

"Yes, yes, it will. Thank you so much."

"You're welcome." Levi held his glass up to toast. "Here's to new alliances."

Penny raised her glass and he clicked his against it, never taking his eyes off her as he took a sip of his wine.

* * *

They made small talk all through supper, and when they finished eating, Penny excused herself to go to the ladies' room. Levi rose to show respect for her as she stood. There was a loud thud as her purse, which had been resting on her lap, fell to the floor. Levi quickly knelt to retrieve it for her and saw the clutch had come open. The white ivory grip of a Colt pistol stuck out of the opening. He casually pushed the gun back into her purse and snapped it closed as he picked it up. He handed it to Penny, giving away nothing.

As she walked away, he wondered why Penny would be carrying a gun. He had never seen a high-society girl carry a gun. *There's a lot more to this woman than meets the eye.*

The small band in the corner began playing. When Penny returned, they sipped their wine and tapped their toes to the music. He watched her across the table, pleased to know she enjoyed music as much as he did. The band began playing "There Never Was a Girl Like You" and he couldn't resist the urge to hold her in his arms.

He rose from his chair and held his palm out to her. "Miss Juzan, would you join me in this dance?"

Penny hesitated for a moment but eventually placed her clutch purse on the table and rose to join him. They walked only a dozen feet to the dance floor and Levi wrapped his arm around her waist. He swore he could feel the electricity flowing between their palms, even through her white gloves. He looked down at her and smiled. She, however, kept her eyes hidden below the brim of her hat. He could tell she was eyeing the table and her purse resting there. He spun her around again and again, but her eyes never strayed from the table.

When the song ended, she said, "I'm feeling a little tired, Levi. If you'd like to walk on the beach, we should go and do that now."

He nodded and escorted her back to the table to retrieve her wrap and clutch, and they exited the dining room through the patio doors. Levi thought back to New Year's Eve and remembered emerging onto the very same patio and locking eyes with Penny for the very first time. She held his arm as they climbed down the sweeping staircase, and when they reached the powdery white sand, she removed her hat so it wouldn't blow away in the wind. Her hair was easing out of its bun and ringlets were softly blowing around her face. Levi couldn't take his eyes off her.

"Oh, this is where they found that poor girl," she said.

"Yes, it's such a shame that incident ruined this area of the beach for so many people."

She looked up at him strangely, and he realized his comment may have been insensitive.

"I mean, too bad for the poor girl and for her family."

After a few minutes of walking in silence, they stopped and turned toward the water. The full moon hung low in the sky, like a picture in a fairy tale.

"It's beautiful," Penny said.

"Not as beautiful as you," Levi countered, turning toward her.

Penny didn't look back at him. He wanted to kiss her, but he could tell by her stiff posture she would not allow him to do so, so he turned and looked back at the white light floating across the black sea.

"So, tell me, why are you here, Mr. Temple?" she asked, eyes still on the water.

"I'm taking a holiday. I rather enjoy hobnobbing with the rich and famous, don't you?"

"Well, yes, of course, but don't you have family back in New York or somewhere?"

"No, I'm an orphan."

"You're a little old to be an orphan." Penny laughed.

"I don't have any family. My parents are both deceased and I have no siblings. That makes me an orphan."

"I guess it does, doesn't it?"

She took his arm and they continued their walk.

After a moment, he asked, "Why are you here, Penny?"

"The same as you, I guess. Just taking a holiday."

"There's a rumor going around that you're here looking for a rich husband."

She stopped and turned toward him, her face turning red with anger. "I beg your pardon, Mr. Temple; I don't need a rich husband. I have as much money as most of these cads. And whoever is spreading those kinds of rumors are not gentlemen but rakes and scoundrels." She unlocked her arm from his and began walking again.

"I'm sorry, Penny. I didn't mean to upset you." He didn't say anything else, thinking he should let her cool off, though it was nice to see she had a little fire in her. He glanced at her out of the corner of his eye and grinned at her anger.

"I'd like to go back," she announced and abruptly changed directions without waiting for a response.

When they reached the path that led back to the annex, Penny wrapped her arms around his and said, "I didn't mean to get angry. I just wish people would mind their own business. I'm not here to find a rich husband, and shame on anyone for saying such an awful thing behind my back."

Levi kept walking slowly toward the annex. She placed her temple on his shoulder and he leaned over and kissed the top of her head. Her hair smelled like vanilla.

Confession

After her moonlit promenade with Levi, Penny entered her apartment to a furious Luke.

"Where have you been?" Luke demanded.

"I really don't think that's any of your business, but if you must know, I had supper with Mr. Temple and then we went for a stroll down the beach." Penny tossed her hat and shawl on the chair and placed her purse on the coffee table. She went into the kitchen to make herself a cup of tea.

Luke followed her. "Don't you know that man is dangerous?"

"Really, Luke, I have it all under control."

"Ending up dead on a beach like one of those servant girls is not having it all under control."

"What makes you think I'll end up dead on the beach?"

"Don't you think he's the one who killed those girls?"

Penny stood silent and thought about it. Finally

she said, "Yes, I think he's the one who killed those girls." After a moment, she continued, "But I need to find what I came here for, and I'm not going to find it if I don't make friends with him."

Luke stomped out of the kitchen, and after Penny poured her tea, she found him sitting on the sofa, staring into the fireplace. She could have sworn he was pouting.

"Luke, are you all right?"

"I'm worried about you."

She shook her head in exasperation. "We've already been through this."

Luke lowered his voice. "I know." He paused. "But there's something I haven't told you."

Penny sat down, took a sip of her tea, and waited for him to continue.

"Penny, I've known you since the day you were born. When your grandma Marguerite left Lake Juzan after your grandpa died, she took my mother with her to Vicksburg. My mother was a three-year-old orphan and your father was two. They grew up as siblings. Your grandma Marguerite raised them together."

"I know all this, Luke. What's your point?"

"My point is, your grandma was trying to escape the curse that killed our grandfathers and great-grandfathers. All of them. Penny, they died for the very thing you're trying to find." He paused and awaited a response, but Penny sipped her tea and didn't say anything, so he continued. He talked about his mother never marrying and giving birth to him out of wedlock, how Penny's father never threw Luke's mother out of the house, how Luke and Penny had also grown up as siblings. "I never thought about it much at the time, but looking back, I guess I always considered your father to be my father, too."

Penny held her teacup between her hands. The memories Luke was dragging up were so sad, and she found it difficult to move or breathe. The warmth of the teacup was comforting. She didn't say anything and let him continue.

"So, out of respect for your father, I've tried to ignore my feelings. I pushed them away for years and years, but after you left last year to go on this treasure hunt, I missed you so much. I didn't understand it myself, but I was afraid you were going to come to the same fate as everyone else who got mixed up with this curse. I realized about a month ago that I'd been denying my feelings for you for a very, very long time. Probably my whole life."

He looked at the floor and took a deep breath. "Our parents are all gone and neither of us have any siblings, so we don't have any family but each other. I don't want you to think of me as a brother. I can't deny my feelings for you any longer."

He fell to his knees in front of her, took the teacup out of her hands, and placed it on the coffee table. He looked up into her eyes and said, "I'm in love with you, Penelope Juzan. I've been in love with you my whole life."

He waited for her to say something.

"That's impossible, Luke. You can't be in love with me. I'm like your sister."

"But you're not my sister."

"We grew up together. We slept in the same bed. We bathed together as children, for Christ's sake."

"That's why I've denied my feelings for you for so long. But there's no one left in the whole wide world that would care if we were together. We can be together now."

She didn't respond, so he rose to his feet and sat back down on the sofa. "You know we've been connected for generations. Our great-grandfathers were best friends—"

"Best friends who killed each other," Penny pointed out.

"That was the curse and you know it. Before that, they were best friends for at least thirty years. Our grandfathers were also best friends."

"That didn't end so well, either."

"The curse again. But our parents were like brother and sister. Your dad loved my mother, so did your mom, and they loved me, too. They never made me feel like I was anything but family.

"Penny, we *are* family, you and I, and I don't want anything to happen to you. I'm afraid for you, for what you're doing with this Levi character. I love you, and I want you to come home with me. Forget about this whole thing. Let's go home before the curse strikes again."

"Luke, I'm well aware of how deep our roots go, and I love you, too, but not romantically. I love you like a brother. I cannot accept your affection. I'm sorry. As far as forgetting this quest and going home, I've searched for a whole year. I've sold everything my family has ever owned just to be in this world, trying to find him. This"—she waved her hands around the ornate room—"isn't cheap. My family's money is all gone. Our beautiful plantation is gone. My home—*our* home—it's been sold so I can do this." She reached over and caressed his shoulder, then rubbed her palm over his black silky hair. "I've found him, Luke. He has what belongs to my family, what belongs to me, and

I'm going to get it back. We can then buy our home back and never have to worry again."

Luke sat back on his heels and looked at her with a pained expression. "You're playing a dangerous game with him, Penny." He looked down. "I want to go back to the way things used to be. I want to take you home."

"Home to what? The plantation was losing money when I sold it. I don't think we would have been able to hang on to it for very much longer at the rate we were going. It's gone now; there's no home to return to. There's nowhere for us to go and nothing we can do until I get back what's rightfully mine, and I'm going to do that very soon. I appreciate you wanting to be here and take care of me, but I want you to leave so I can concentrate on what I need to do here."

She looked into the fire. "Besides, I don't believe in curses."

After a few moments of silence, she added, "And I think I have a plan."

Changing Tides

The sun was just beginning to rise as Penny and Charles planted themselves in the duck blind behind some brush on the far side of the game preserve, only yards from a small pond. The light sparkled on the surface and the seabirds whistled as they flew inland for fresh water. After her conversation with Luke, Penny had stayed up most of the night planning her next move. She remained silent next to Charles as she reviewed and revised it in her head. When she was certain she had thought through all the possible outcomes and knew the plan would work, she put it into action.

"Charles, what do you know about Levi Temple?"

Charles gazed across the pond and shook his head. "Not very much, I'm afraid. He was a business partner of your uncle's, and he said he came here for the season to escape the dreariness of winter in the city. Why do you ask?"

"I'm just wondering. I notice little things in his behavior and dress and wonder if he really is who he says he is."

"What do you mean?"

"Oh, it's nothing really, but sometimes he dresses strangely, and occasionally he says or does things that are slightly inappropriate. It's nothing that would really stick out if you weren't looking for it, but it seems he's trying so hard to be one of us. I also get the impression he's watching us all the time, like he's studying us or something. It's a little creepy."

"Well, now that you mention it, he is quite a strange fellow."

Charles blew the duck call and the two waited in silence. When no ducks heeded the call right away, Charles continued, "I know what you mean about his inappropriate behavior. When I heard he gutted that quail right in front of everyone, I was shocked. Why would someone do such a thing?"

"I don't know. That's why I asked you about him."

"Well, let me have my people look into him. If he is who he says he is, we should find lots of records for art purchases he made for your uncle."

She sighed. "All right. That would make me feel better."

Charles blew the call again and a small flock of black ducks rose from the other side of the field and headed directly toward them. They drew their guns and waited until the ducks were within firing range. Charles fired and missed. Penny fired and felled a bird.

Charles laughed. "Well, Miss Juzan, what I heard about you is true. You're a crack shot!"

Penny smiled. "Oh, it was just dumb luck."

The two hunted for the rest of the morning and returned to the club with three ducks, all shot by Penny. After they dropped them off at the taxidermist, Charles said, "It was a great pleasure hunting with you this morning. We should do it again real soon, and I'll check into that topic we discussed and let you know what I find out."

"Thank you, Charles. It would satisfy my curiosity to know something either way." She turned away but quickly turned back. "Oh, and thank you for taking me hunting."

He smiled and nodded.

She walked across the sandy grass toward the annex.

When she arrived, she found her suite empty. Luke's belongings were gone. She breathed a sigh of relief. "In love with me—pshaw," she mumbled. "How can I focus on what I need to do with him loitering around? Thank goodness he had the sense to leave before he ruined everything."

With the weight of her childhood friend hiding in her suite lifted off her shoulders, she napped, then she bathed and primped and adorned herself in a most elegant turquoise satin dress for supper at the club. She spun around in the full-length mirror, admiring the back of her dress, which had lace trailing from the shoulders to the floor in the shape and color of peacock feathers. She tied the matching turquoise sash around her waist and wrapped a shawl around her shoulders and pranced over to the club. She had a renewed spring in her step and knew she had a sparkle in her eye. She wanted to put the rest of her plan into action and needed to run into Nelson during the evening to do so.

As she waited in the entryway for the maître d'

to ready her table, Nelson approached her. "Good evening, Miss Juzan. How are you this evening?"

"I'm fine, Nelson, and how are you?"

"I'm afraid my dinner companions are in the middle of a death match game of chess, so it looks like I'll be dining all alone this evening. Would you care to join me?"

"Oh, that would be very nice. I'd love to."

The maître d' showed them to a small linen-covered table for two on the farthest side of the dining room.

As they enjoyed roasted duck and white wine, the two chatted about the weather, the island, and croquet. Eventually the conversation turned to hunting. Penny took the opportunity to mention that she and Charles had gone duck hunting that morning, and she relayed the conversation she'd had with Charles regarding Levi Temple.

"Well, I think you're correct. There is something a little different about him, but I think he's a fine chap, don't you?"

"You do? I'm not so sure. I mean, where did he come from? Why haven't we heard of him before now? And why are there suddenly dead servants in our midst?"

Nelson froze. His face turned pale and a bead of perspiration appeared on his upper lip. "You don't really think Levi had anything to do with those girls, do you?"

"No, well, maybe. We don't really know anything about him, do we?"

"I'm sure the sheriff has talked with him."

"Yes, I'm sure he has, but his alibi for last weekend was that he was home alone and drunk."

"That's not much of an alibi." Nelson held his wineglass by the stem and twisted it around and around. The waiter came over with a carafe of wine and offered to refill the empty glass, but Nelson and Penny shook their heads and the waiter disappeared.

"No, it's not an alibi at all, and I wonder what kind of man sits around all alone getting drunk. Wouldn't he want some company?" Penny looked at him slyly. "Maybe some female company?"

Nelson stopped spinning his glass and placed it down on the table. "Miss Juzan, I'm afraid that's quite a serious accusation."

"Don't get me wrong, Nelson. I like the man as much as everyone else. I just wonder about the coincidence of his arrival and the discovery of the first servant girl, and now his weak alibi and the discovery of the second servant girl." Penny shook her head and waved her hand in front of her face. "Oh, never mind me. I'm just being silly, letting my imagination run wild. Of course Levi wouldn't do such a thing. I'm sure the sheriff will find out who the murderer is very soon." She took a sip of her wine and watched Nelson's expression.

He put a faint smile on his face, but she could tell his mind was racing with the possibility that Levi Temple might be the murderer. He was distant for the remainder of the meal, and as soon as they finished eating, he excused himself and made a hurried escape.

She soundlessly followed him across the club's lawn and down the road to Charles's front door. She hid behind the large holly shrub and watched as Charles invited Nelson into the house. She was pleased. Charles and Nelson were now suspicious of Levi and his world would soon begin to unravel. It was a good thing he had her to turn to when his high-society friends abandoned him. Of course she would be there to comfort him and soothe his wounds.

She strolled back to her suite, enjoying the balmy breeze and admiring the twinkling stars.

Shunned

Levi spent the next few days wandering around the club, wondering where his new friends had disappeared to. He checked the tennis court, the billiard room, the croquet lawn, and even asked the taxidermist if he had seen Nelson or Charles, but Bernie said he hadn't seen them in a few days. It was as if they had vanished into thin air.

Fortunately, there was a cocktail party being held at the club starting at five p.m., and Levi was sure everyone would be in attendance. He dressed in his finest jacket and tie and ventured to the club. When he reached the entry, the doorman told him his presence was urgently requested in Charles's office.

With a bit of confusion, he walked down the long hallway and found a door sporting a brass plaque that read PRESIDENT. He lightly rapped on the door and heard Charles bellow from within, "Come in."

Levi cracked open the door and stuck his head in. "Hello, Charles. You wanted to see me?"

Charles looked up from his seat behind a massive mahogany desk. His expression was neither warm nor friendly.

"Mr. Temple, please come in and have a seat," Charles said as he placed his pen in its holder.

Levi entered the office and found the chairs filled with J.P., John Sr., Nelson, and Penny's friend, George Turner. He nodded at the men but they did not return the greeting. The heat of anxiety traveled up his spine and set off a sudden throbbing in his temples.

"Please sit." Charles gestured toward a chair in the middle of the group.

"What's going on here?" Levi asked.

"Well, that's precisely what we'd like to ask you, Mr. Temple," said Charles.

"I'm sure I don't know what you mean. And why are you calling me Mr. Temple? I thought we were friends." He looked around at each stern face staring back at him. "I thought we were all friends."

"We have a little problem. You see, I called Cornelius Bliss's widow and it seems she's never heard of you. How do you explain that?"

Levi shook his head. "It doesn't surprise me that Mary doesn't know me. I've never met the woman face to face. All of the transactions Cornelius and I did were strictly for his art collection. He said his wife was not interested in such things. I mostly traveled back and forth to France to procure works for him by Claude Monet, and I worked with an artist in New York by the name of Arthur Bowen Davies."

"I thought Mary gave you the key to the apartment," said Charles.

"Actually, it was her assistant who gave me the key." Levi stared at Charles and didn't blink an eye, hoping the woman actually had an assistant.

The men looked at each other.

Nelson spoke up. "Levi, which paintings by Monet did you acquire for Mr. Bliss?"

Without hesitation, Levi answered, "One was the *Manneporte near Étretat*. I don't really know what Cornelius saw in the painting. It looked like a big rock sticking up out of the water to me. But for some reason, he loved it and had to have it so I made sure he got it."

Nelson's expression softened as he looked at Charles and Levi. When Charles didn't respond, Nelson spoke again. "Perhaps we've been a little hasty in our judgments, Levi. Will you please excuse us and go enjoy the cocktail party?"

Levi nodded, rose from the chair, and left the room. He closed the door behind him. *Whew, that was close. At least Nelson seems to be on my side.*

* * *

On the other side of the door, the men debated the veracity of Levi's answers.

"How would he know about the painting if he wasn't the one who purchased it?" Nelson asked.

"Anyone with access to the society pages would know about the painting, Nelson. Every time we move or breathe, someone is writing about it. Don't be so naive," Charles snapped. "I am the president of this club, and as such, I have a responsibility to maintain the integrity of its membership. I'm not yet convinced that Mr. Temple is who he says he is."

He looked at George. "George, will you reach your people in New York and dig up this Arthur

Davies? Let's see if he knows Mr. Temple."

George nodded.

Charles looked from face to face. "The rest of you will keep this under wraps until we get to the bottom of it, and keep your eyes on Mr. Temple."

* * *

Levi headed to the nearest bar and ordered a whiskey, straight up. He thanked the bartender and downed the drink in one gulp. He grimaced as it burned the back of his throat, and then placed the empty glass on the bar and said, "Another, please." He picked up the refilled glass and realized the whiskey was the remedy for his throbbing head because he felt better already. He turned and scanned the room, and his eyes immediately fell on Penny, who was standing in the corner speaking with a couple of suited gentlemen. His eyes locked with hers and Levi felt a surge of heat run up the back of his neck like flames in dry tinder, but this time it was a good feeling. He didn't know if it was the effects of the whiskey or the mere sight of her, but whatever it was, he liked it. He downed the second glass of whiskey and without hesitation, marched straight toward her.

With no greeting or smile, he grabbed her upper arm and said, "I need to speak with you in private."

She awkwardly excused herself from the men and walked out the nearest door with Levi still pulling her arm.

When they were alone in the garden, she pulled away from his grasp. "What is wrong with you? You seem...edgy."

"Edgy is a good word, I guess. I was just called

into Charles's office and questioned about my relationship with Cornelius. It was extremely rude of him and very frustrating for me."

"Why would he question you about something like that?"

"I have no idea. It was certainly uncalled for. I was having a great season here but now I'm thinking I should leave."

"Leave? You can't leave. We're just getting to know each other."

"That is precisely what's bothering me."

They looked into each other's eyes for a few minutes. He really wanted to kiss her, but out here in the garden under the windows of a full dining room probably wasn't the place.

Tears came to Penny's eyes. "I'll miss you if you go."

"I'll miss you, too. Why don't you come with me? We'll travel the world together." Levi smiled at the thought of a great adventure with a stunning woman. "I may know a yacht that's for sale. Would you like that?"

"A yacht? I don't think I'd be comfortable on a yacht. I like dry land better."

"Well, how about France? France is full of dry land. Would you like to go there?"

"Um, Levi, this is moving far too quickly for me. I need more time to get to know you before I'd even consider running off with you. Really, you're still a stranger to me."

"I'm not a stranger."

"Yes, you are. I hardly know anything about you."

"What do you want to know? Just ask."

"Okay, where do you live?"

"I have an apartment in New York on Fifth Avenue."

"Where were you born?"

"Lauderdale County, Mississippi."

"What were your parents' names?"

"My father was Thomas Stuc...Temple. My mother's name was, um, Mary." He recovered quickly. "What else do you want to know?"

"Levi, I can't just disappear with you into the blue." She looked off into the distance for a moment and then turned back to him. "And how could we afford to go to France? Do you have that kind of money that we could just up and leave like that?"

Levi slowed his breathing. He had almost blown it. He needed to maintain control of his emotions. He'd never had a problem with control before, but this woman ignited some kind of fire in him that he had no experience with. He took both of her hands. "Yes, Penny, I have enough money. I have plenty of money." He smiled at her.

She smiled back. "Well, let me think about this for a few days. I would really like to get to know you better before I make that kind of decision."

"Then have a private supper with me tonight. We can spend the evening at my apartment and get to know each other."

Penny paused for a moment then nodded.

"Good. I'll arrange for supper and pick you up at your suite at seven o'clock." He lifted her hands to his lips and softly kissed them one at a time. "Until then, *mon cheri*."

Privacy

Levi knocked on Penny's door promptly at seven o'clock and escorted her down the stairs to his apartment.

"Have you been here before?" Levi asked.

"No, I haven't. My uncle told me all about it, though."

"Why are you staying in a suite instead of here?" he asked as he took her hand and led her to the dining table.

"I forgot to ask my aunt for the key at the funeral and didn't want to go back and bother her in her time of grief." She looked at the lavish banquet spread across the rich burgundy damask tablecloth. "This is lovely, Levi. Thank you for inviting me."

"You're quite welcome." He pulled out her chair for her then walked around the table to his seat.

"Would you care for some wine?" he asked,

pulling a bottle of wine from an ice bucket next to the table.

"Yes, please."

After filling the glasses, he raised his and said, "How about a toast?"

She held up her glass.

"To new beginnings."

They drank, gazing over the rims at each other. He placed his glass down, folded his hands under his chin, and stared at her.

"What are you looking at?" She blushed.

"You. You are the most beautiful woman I have ever seen."

She grinned at him.

After a moment, he tore his eyes away from hers and made a grand display of lifting the silver lids from their plates. He uncovered steaks and lobster tails laid out in perfect proportion on white bone china, and he looked at her for her approval. She nodded and smiled. He picked up his knife and cut into his rare steak, watching the blood pool around the lobster tails. He then looked back at her. "Now, tell me about yourself. Where were you born?"

"I was born in Vicksburg, Mississippi."

"Do you still live there?"

"Yes, but my family was originally from just north of Lauderdale County."

Levi stopped chewing and looked at her. "Lauderdale County?"

"Yes, my family is from Lake Juzan."

"Oh, I didn't even put that together. With a name like Juzan, that would make sense, now wouldn't it? I've never been to the lake but I've heard of it."

"It's a beautiful area."

"Why don't you live there anymore?"

Penny sipped her wine and blotted her lips with the napkin. "Well, that's a long story. My great-grandfather owned an inn on the lake, but sadly, he drowned in that very lake."

"We have more in common than you know. My father owned an inn on the Chunky River. I believe that river flows out of Lake Juzan."

"Yes, I think it does."

"How did your great-grandfather drown?"

"He was in the middle of the lake in a rowboat and his boot lace got caught on something heavy and pulled him under."

"Oh, that's horrible. What about your grandparents and parents?"

"My grandfather died in the lake, too. He didn't drown, though; he was bitten by a cottonmouth. The bite was fatal. My grandmother found him floating in the lake. She then took my father, who was a baby at the time, and moved to Vicksburg. She said there was some kind of curse around that lake and she wanted to get away from it."

"That's an interesting story. I guess with losing your great-grandfather and your grandfather, I can understand why she'd think there might be a curse. I've never heard of a curse surrounding that lake, though."

"Well, maybe it's a family curse. I don't know. Anyway, when my father, Theodore Juzan, grew up, he married my mother, Betty, and they had me. I was an only child. I grew up in Vicksburg on an eight-hundred-acre plantation on the Mississippi River. My father died in 1901 and my mother died just a couple years ago."

"Yet more coincidences. My father died in 1901 also. I didn't have a mother around, though. I've taken care of myself ever since."

"You were awfully young in 1901 to be on your own. What happened to your father's inn?"

"I don't rightly know. I left town immediately after he died. Haven't been back since."

"You just walked away and left everything?"

"Pretty much. I took some clothes and his money, of course."

"He must have left you a lot of money if you've been living off it for ten years."

"He had enough. I'm comfortable." He smiled at her and took a long drink of his wine.

She sipped her wine also and they sat in silence for a few minutes.

"So, Levi, how much is enough?"

"How much what?" He cut another piece of steak.

"How much money? How much is enough?"

He thought about it for a moment. "Truthfully, I don't know. I'm beginning to think it's more important to be respected, to be an upstanding member of society, than to have money. I've found being a member of this group here on the island to be more rewarding than monetary wealth."

"But you can't be a member of this group without wealth."

"True, and look around. It's nice, don't you agree?"

She grinned and nodded.

"I guess we'll just have to settle for the best of everything—money *and* status."

Following their candlelight supper, Levi lit a fire and asked Penny if she'd like to move into the living room and continue their conversation.

She sat on the sofa across from the blazing fire and Levi sat next to her. They stared into the flames as their conversation waned. After a few minutes, he looked at her. She was stunning even in profile, with her dainty, pointed chin and the slightest tilt to her nose. She looked back at him and her green eyes hypnotized him. He leaned forward and kissed her full lips. She allowed him to kiss her. She smelled like the soap he had smelled on her the day they went quail hunting. He hadn't been able to put his finger on the scent at the time, but now identified it as a mix of lavender and vanilla. He wrapped his hand behind her neck and pulled her closer. She melted into his arms, and as the fire crackled in the distance, they continued their kiss.

He's Back

Later that evening, Levi walked Penny back to her suite and kissed her good night in the hallway in front of her door, promising he'd see her again the next day. With a smile, she assured him she was already looking forward to it. She entered her suite and turned the lock, listening through the door to the echo of his boots as he walked away. When she was sure he was gone, she turned on the light in the dining room, and jumped when she saw someone standing silently in the darkness of the kitchen.

"Dammit, why do you always do that?" she said, taking a deep breath, her hand clutching her throat.

"Do you know what time it is?"

"What?"

"Do you know what time it is?" Luke repeated, like a father reprimanding a teenage daughter.

"No, I don't," she snapped as she marched into the living room and sat on the sofa to remove her shoes.

"It's three o'clock in the morning, Penny. Were you with him?"

"If you mean Levi, yes, I was. What's it to you and why are you here? I thought you left."

"I couldn't leave." Luke sat next to her. "I tried to sneak aboard the ferry boat a couple times but couldn't get on without being seen so I had to come back."

"Well, you can't stay here. You have to go, Luke."

"Why? So you can fall in love with him?"

She rose from the sofa and placed her hands on her hips. "Don't be stupid. I'm not going to fall in love with him, but I need to get close so I can claim what's rightfully mine."

Luke didn't move. He gazed at her like a lovesick teenager. She ignored his expression.

"I'm sure I'm on the right path. Tonight I learned everything I needed to know."

"Like what?"

"Well, for one thing, I asked him who his father was and he almost said Thomas Stuckey. He caught himself and hurriedly said his father was Thomas Temple. And during supper, he told me his father owned an inn and that he died in 1901. That's the exact information I got from the Lauderdale County sheriff. Sheriff Temple told me Thomas Stuckey had an inn on the river and was hung in 1901 for murdering his guests. The day he was hung, his son Levi disappeared without a trace. Levi told me when his father died, he left the inn and never returned. The sheriff said the boy was about twelve years old at the time. That was ten years ago and Levi is twenty two, so I'm one hundred percent positive I have the right man."

"So, how do you know he still has the trunk?"

"Two reasons. First, the sheriff gave me a list of known victims from Stuckey's inn. My father's friend, Carter Stuckey, was on that list. If Carter stopped at that inn for the night, he would have had the trunk with him, and if he was killed by Thomas Stuckey, the trunk would then be in Thomas's possession. The sheriff said after the hanging they searched the property and found nothing of value. Which means Levi took the trunk when he left.

"The inn was auctioned off a couple years ago and when I was in Lauderdale County, I went there to speak with the new owner. He told me they had a lot of things to clean out before they could move in, and they went over every inch of the property. There was nothing of value, only mismatched household furnishings, a broken-down horse corral, and a few rabbit hutches behind the barn. No trunk. And the other day, Levi said something strange about his fortune coming from an old trunk full of gold. Who makes a joke like that? Too much coincidence to think he doesn't have the trunk."

"What's the second reason?"

"Where do you think he gets all the money to live a lavish lifestyle like this? I've had to sell off everything my family has ever owned just to travel for a year to find him. Staying here on Jekyll Island for the last few weeks has cost a small fortune. He's been living this lifestyle for ten years."

Luke nodded. "So, what's your plan?"

"I'm going to be as sweet as sugar to him and get him to tell me where the trunk is. Then I'm going to take it back."

"Do you think it'll be that simple?"

Penny lifted her skirt up to her thigh and pulled her pistol from her garter. "If not, we'll go with plan B."

Insult and Retribution

Levi woke to a cool overcast day and decided it was perfect weather to go hunting. He dressed and went upstairs to knock on Penny's door to see if she would like to accompany him. He waited for a few moments but she didn't answer. He knocked again with the same result. He wondered if she had already gone to the club for breakfast and decided to go there and check.

He thought it strange that he felt so wonderful. He never remembered feeling this way before. He strutted across the lawn and bounced up the stairs of the club with a renewed sense of vigor and enthusiasm about life. If he didn't know better, he would think the feeling was none other than being in love. He smiled at the thought. Well, why not?

He nodded to the doorman, greeted the maître d' with a hearty "Good morning!" and stuck his head in the dining room to look for Penny. Yes, she was there, seated in the corner all by herself. Levi advanced toward the table but was rudely cut off by none other than George Turner. Levi stopped in mid-stride to avoid being knocked down by the man as he hurried past Levi toward Penny's table. Levi wondered why Penny was having breakfast with George.

George kissed Penny on the cheek and said, "Sorry I'm late."

"Oh, that's no problem," Penny crooned, with a smile that was as delightful as that of a young girl in love.

Levi hated the way she looked at the man. He felt his ears grow hot and the fire of jealousy rumble in his stomach. He would like to pick George Turner up by his shirt collar and throw him out the nearest window. How dare he move in on Penny?

Suddenly aware that Penny may glance over and see him standing there, Levi backed up a few steps. He had to escape the dining room immediately before he did something he would regret. He wouldn't cause a scene right now, but he was certain that George Turner would soon pay for this misdeed. *These high-society types think they can simply take everything they want. But George Turner has chosen the wrong thing to take.*

Penny was not available for the taking.

* * *

That night, Levi stood next to a giant palm tree. The small sliver of moon didn't cast much light and the overcast day had transformed into a clear night. He leaned against the tree and watched a lamp glow behind the sheer curtains of the second-floor window. Fireflies danced on the lawn, katydids buzzed in the trees, a cat weaved in and out of the bushes lining the front of the house and meowed a few times. Levi scowled. He never did like cats and he was losing patience with the upstairs lamp. He wished it would turn off already.

He had followed the man home that evening from the club and watched the lights radiate from the first-floor windows for more than an hour. After those were turned off, the lamp in the upstairs window had been illuminated, and Levi was sure the house would go completely dark shortly but it hadn't. For two more hours the lamp had remained aglow in the upstairs window. The man must have been reading or maybe he'd fallen asleep with the lamp on. Levi would wait for a little while longer. There was no sense walking into an altercation when the passage of time was all that was needed to prevent one.

Levi dug his silver lighter out of his pocket and repeatedly flipped it open and closed, never pushing the ignition button. He looked around at the shadows covering the property, and from what he could tell, it was quite beautiful and exquisitely landscaped. It was not far from the game preserve, and he'd bet one could shoot a deer or a turkey right from the front porch. He would like to have a house like this one day. Maybe he should just take this one. He grinned, flipped the lighter open and closed again, and looked over his shoulder. The road behind him was dark. He hadn't seen a soul since he left the club. No one would venture this far away from the center of the island and the hub of excitement, so Levi didn't need to worry about being seen.

He looked back up at the lit window and pouted. He hated waiting, but he would wait all night if that's what it took. The cat meowed again. Levi sneered at it.

He saw the patch of light from the window disappear and glanced up. The window was black. Time to go to work. He placed the lighter back in his pocket and unbuckled his belt. He slid it out of the belt loops and wrapped it around the knuckles of his right hand. He looked at it, wondering if punching someone with a belt around his knuckles would do as much damage as punching someone with a bare fist. It certainly would protect his knuckles. He'd have to remember that.

He hunched down and crept toward the porch. He passed the meowing cat and tiptoed up the steps. He turned the brass handle of the front door. It was unlocked. He entered the house, looked back again at the road to make sure no one saw him, and softly closed the door. The latch produced the faintest click. He froze and listened for any movement from upstairs. There was none.

He looked around and got his bearings. Parlor to the left, kitchen to the right, stairway straight ahead. He moved toward the stairway and stepped up onto the first step. The boards creaked. He froze again. The house remained silent. He viewed the thirteen steps rising in front of him and thought if they all creaked like the first one did, it would take a long time to climb the staircase. He prayed the man was a sound sleeper. He took the next step. Silence. And the third. No more creaking. He let out a small sigh of relief. When he reached the top landing, he moved toward the room that had previously been aglow. The door was closed. He placed his left hand on the knob and slowly turned it.

The room was dark but Levi saw the large black shadow of the bed to his right. He took a step in that direction and was grabbed around the neck by someone behind the door. The assailant shoved Levi to the floor and quickly got on top of him. Levi punched toward where he assumed a face would be and made contact with something firm. With the leather belt still wrapped around his hand, his knuckles didn't ache when they hit their target, so Levi punched again and again, making contact every time. His attacker weakened and Levi flipped him over, sitting on top of the man who had now gone limp. Levi unwrapped the belt from his knuckles and slid it under the man's neck. He pulled as tight as he could until he was sure the man was no longer breathing.

In the stillness, Levi recognized his attacker as George Turner. He stood and put his belt back on. He left George sprawled in the middle of the floor and proceeded to destroy everything in the house. He knocked over lamps and pushed knickknacks off tables. He grabbed paintings from the walls and smashed their frames. He wished he could go through the items piece by piece and see if there was anything he'd like to own, but he didn't have time for that, and he didn't want anyone to see him in the possession of items belonging to a dead man.

After destroying the upstairs bedrooms, he went into the kitchen, opened the cabinets, and began breaking the crystal stemware and bone china.

"That man doesn't deserve any of this," he mumbled as objects crashed to the floor around him. "He should know better than to try and steal another man's property." He smashed a plate. "Especially another man's woman." He smashed the soup tureen.

Broken fragments crunched under his feet as he exited the kitchen and entered the parlor. He stacked logs and kindling into the fireplace and lit them with his silver lighter. He watched them catch fire and begin to burn. He stared into the fire, reliving the brawl that had just happened upstairs. He reached up and touched his eye. It was already beginning to swell and he knew it would be bruised by morning. He was surprised George had heard him enter the house. He was sure he'd been quiet. *Oh, well.* He shook his head. *Knowledge doesn't always win. Sometimes brute strength does.*

He took a burning branch from the fireplace and placed it on the rug in front of the sofa. Quickly, the rug caught fire and the flames spread to the sofa. Satisfied that his job was done, Levi left the house and closed the front door. The cat meowed at him as he stepped off the front porch.

He was asleep in the cozy bed of his apartment long before anyone smelled smoke from the far side of the island.

Island Uproar

Levi was enjoying breakfast alone at a table in the back of the Grand Dining Room when he saw Penny nearly running through the crowd, heading straight toward him.

"Did you hear what happened last night?" she said when she reached his table. "Everyone is talking about it."

He rose, kissed her cheek, and pulled out a chair so she could join him. "No, my dear, what happened last night?"

She gawked at him. "What happened to your eye?"

He softly touched his blackened eye, wincing a bit. "I walked straight into the bedroom door last night." He shook his head. "I should have turned on a light when I got up in the middle of the night. I didn't realize the door was half closed and I slammed right into it."

"It looks painful."

He gave her a reassuring smile. "It's not as bad as it looks. Now, tell me, what happened last night? Something exciting, I hope."

Her eyes brimmed with tears. "My dear friend George Turner died in a house fire."

"A house fire?" Levi raised his eyebrows.

"Yes, his house burned down last night with him inside."

"Oh, that's horrible, my dear. Who told you this?"

"Charles and Nelson. Charles said he woke in the middle of the night and smelled smoke. He went to Nelson's house and together they grabbed a couple horses and rode around the island until they found the fire. Nelson said there was nothing but smoldering rubble by the time they arrived. The house was completely burned to the ground, nothing left standing but the brick chimney."

"How do you know your friend was in the house?"

"They said they looked everywhere for him. He's nowhere to be found. He must have been sleeping when the fire broke out."

"That's so sad, Penny. I'm very sorry." Levi sipped his coffee.

The waiter came to the table with a fresh pot of coffee and Penny nodded to him that she would like some.

"Would you like to order something, ma'am?" the waiter asked Penny as he filled her cup and placed some fresh croissants in the center of the table.

She shook her head and reached for one of the croissants and placed it on her bread plate. She took a sip of her coffee and closed her eyes as she swallowed. She looked as if the hot liquid was soothing away the horror of the previous night's events. She was beautiful in her floppy beach hat and navy blue dress with a little white collar. When she opened her eyes, the sadness that had only moments ago filled them had vanished, and Levi grew suspicious that it was all an act.

"How long have you known poor George?" Levi asked as he scooped some scrambled eggs onto his fork.

"Only since I got here, but he was a very nice man."

Levi took his final bite and pushed his plate away. "Did anyone call the sheriff?"

Penny shook her head. "I don't think so. Why would anyone call the sheriff?"

"Oh, I don't know. I thought you were supposed to report things like that."

Penny shrugged. "Well, I guess if there was foul play or something, but I think he was probably just careless with his fireplace."

Charles and Nelson approached the table. They nodded a greeting to Penny and turned to Levi.

"Mr. Temple, would you please accompany us to my office?" Charles asked.

"Of course, Charles." Levi placed his napkin on the table as he rose. "Would you excuse me, my dear? Enjoy your croissant and I'll be right back."

Penny nodded.

Charles marched through the building and Levi struggled to keep up, following him down the long hallway with the parquet floor. Nelson trailed behind Levi. When they entered the office, Charles walked around his desk and sat in his leather chair. "Have a seat, will you?" He gestured toward the armchair in front of his desk and Levi sat down.

Nelson closed the door and remained standing near it like a sentinel. Levi thought the action very uncharacteristic for Nelson, who had always been warm and cordial.

"What do you know about George Turner?" Charles asked.

"Oh, I just heard his house burned down last night. Have you found him yet? Penny said he may have died in the fire."

"Did you see Mr. Turner last evening?"

"Last evening? No, I didn't. I didn't see anyone. I had supper alone in my apartment."

Charles narrowed his eyes at Levi. "And how did you get that shiner?"

Levi laughed and reached up to touch the bruise. "Oh, it was stupid of me really. I walked into my bedroom door in the middle of the night."

Charles looked down at a piece of paper on his desk, as if uninterested in Levi's answer.

"Charles, why are you asking me questions about George? Do you think he died in the fire?" Levi asked.

"Oh, I'm quite certain of it." Charles held up the piece of paper for Levi to see. "You see this?" He wiggled it. "It's a note from George Turner dated yesterday. I had asked him to have his people contact that artist in New York...what's his name?" He glanced at the paper. "Davies ...Arthur Davies, to see if he remembered you from your alleged art purchases for Cornelius Bliss. This note says George got word from this Arthur Davies yesterday, and he wanted to speak with me this morning about his findings. What do you suppose Mr. Davies had to say about you?"

"I'm sure I wouldn't know. Hopefully he would say I am a fine businessman and discriminating art connoisseur."

"Well, I guess we won't find out today, will we?"

"Really, Charles, I don't know what you're getting at."

Charles rose from his desk, leaned forward, and placed his fingertips on the dark mahogany. He lowered his voice and spoke very slowly. "What I'm getting at, Mr. Temple, is that I'm more and more convinced you're not who you say you are, and as soon as I prove it, I will not only have you thrown off this island, but I won't even offer you a boat ride to the mainland. I'll let you swim."

For a few moments that seemed like an hour, the two stared each other down across the desk. Charles loomed over Levi and Levi struggled to keep his temper in check. How dare this man threaten him? He was certain Charles wouldn't give him the fight George Turner had, but right now wasn't the time to prove that assumption. He wouldn't allow this pasty, sorry excuse for a man to make him lose his composure. Instead, he smiled, and saw Charles's face twitch with confusion and perhaps a touch of anxiety. Levi rose, marched past Nelson without a glance at him, and slammed the door as loudly as he could on his way out.

"And you, Charles, may soon come to the same fate as your dear friend George," Levi muttered as he marched down the front steps, exiting the club.

He completely forgot that he'd left Penny waiting for him in the dining room, and hours later, when she knocked on his apartment door, he had a lot of explaining to do.

Consolation

When Levi heard the knock on his apartment door, he immediately knew who it was and realized what he had done. He jerked the door open and faced a very angry Penny. Her scrunched red face almost made him laugh, but he knew that response would only make her more livid.

"Oh, my dear, I'm so sorry." He reached for her hand and pulled her inside.

She was reluctant but allowed him to pull her into the apartment.

"How could you just leave me sitting in the dining room all by myself?" She looked into his eyes.

"Penny, I am so very sorry. Nelson and Charles made me upset and I wasn't thinking clearly. Can you ever forgive me?" He looked deeply into her emerald eyes. Surprisingly, what he saw wasn't anger but desire. He pulled her into his arms and kissed her passionately.

"Forgive me?"

"Well, all right, if you promise to never do

anything like that again."

"I promise." He kissed her again as he pushed her wrap off her shoulders. He then took her hat and her clutch and dropped them on the table near the door, never taking his eyes off her.

"What is that music I hear?" she asked, her expression softening.

He smiled. "It's an aria from an opera. Do you like it?"

She nodded. "It's beautiful."

He took her by the hand and led her down the hall into the bedroom, where a record was playing on the Victrola. Her jaw dropped when she saw the record player.

"Isn't it beautiful?" he asked. "It probably cost a small fortune."

It was in a Queen Anne-style wooden cabinet with gold trim and had a windup crank on the right side. It wasn't just a record player; it was a piece of furniture. She approached it, listening to the haunting sadness coming from the tapered horn.

"That is the most beautiful song I've ever heard. What's the name of it?" she asked.

"It's from an opera called *Una Furtiva Lagrima*." His Italian was flawless, and by the look on her face, she was impressed. He wrapped his arms around her as the singer sang, *"Una furtiva lagrima negli occhi suoi spunto, quelle festose giovani invidiar sembro."*

Levi began to dance with Penny. "Would you like me to translate?"

She nodded.

He placed his hand on the small of her back and pulled her close. The vanilla smell of her hair took his breath away. As they swayed, he translated.

"A single secret tear from her eye did spring, as if she envied all the youths that laughingly passed her by."

He looked down at Penny and found her eyes closed, as if she was being swept away by the music.

He continued the translation. "What more searching do I need to do? She loves me."

He stopped swaying and she opened her eyes.

"Yes, she loves me."

He melted into her hypnotic stare.

"I see it. I see it."

They gazed into each other's eyes for the remainder of the song, and as the music came to a crescendo, he slowly bent his head and kissed her, wrapping his hand around the back of her neck and pulling her to him as if it were possible for them to become one. He released her hair from its pin and it fell to her waist like a waterfall of sweet-smelling silk. He buried his face in it. He lifted her into his arms and carried her to the bed, where they spent the rest of the day in the pleasure of each other's arms.

As the sun began to set and the hush of darkness crept into the room, Penny propped herself up on her elbow and asked, "What are the rest of the words to that song?"

He gently pushed a stray strand of hair from her face.

"For an instant, the beating of her heart I could feel, as if my sighs were hers and hers were mine." He traced a finger down to her throat and continued further down between her naked breasts, where he felt her heartbeat quicken. She inhaled sharply at his touch. "The beating of her heart I could feel. I could die and ask for nothing more, nothing more. Yes, I could die. I could die of love."

He raised his hand back up to her cheek and ever so softly kissed her lips. He lingered there for as long as she would allow.

Penny traced the line of his jaw with her finger. "It's beautiful."

"Almost as beautiful as you." He pulled her to him and kissed her more deeply. "Would you like to spend the night here with me?"

She smiled. "Yes, I would like that very much."

They made love again.

* * *

Night soon fell and blackness enveloped the room. Penny remained still and listened to Levi's breath. He snored softly as his breathing became more regular. When she was sure he was deeply asleep, she gently kicked the blanket off and rose from the bed. She grabbed his shirt from the floor, wrapped it around her naked body, and tiptoed out of the room.

She turned on the light in the dining room and stopped for a moment, allowing her eyes to adjust to the brightness. The harsh light brought her back to her senses and the reason she was here. She couldn't allow herself to get swept into a romance, but she had loved the aria the moment she entered the apartment. The way he translated the lyrics for her stole her heart. In another time and place, she could love a man like Levi Temple. But Levi Temple didn't exist, did he? She shook her head, attempting to rid herself of her dream. She decided to be in love with the song and not the man. When she retrieved her money from him, the first thing she would buy would be a Victrola and a copy of

Una Furtiva Lagrima.

She turned to look around the room. "Now, if I were hiding a large trunk, where would I hide it?" She opened the closet near the front door. There were coats and umbrellas, a few hats on the shelf, and a box on the floor. She lifted the lid to the box and found it full of gloves and scarfs, but no trunk. She softly closed the door and glanced around the room. There was no other place to store a trunk in the room, so she headed into the kitchen.

She had never actually seen the trunk and didn't know how big it was, so she opened and closed the cabinet doors one at a time but didn't find what she was looking for. She checked the pantry. No trunk.

She checked the bathroom and the other two bedrooms, under the beds, in the closets. No trunk. She paused for a moment to think, staring down at the bed in the final room she checked. It was covered by a red silk duvet, beautiful and expensive, if not a little tacky. She smirked at the color. "Well, the only other place it could be is in the room with him," she whispered.

"In the room with whom?" he asked from behind her.

She spun around and saw him leaning on the door frame, naked as the day he was born, his arms crossed over his muscular chest.

"Oh, I was just looking for something else to wear."

"You look fine in that shirt." He grinned. "If you want a robe or a sweater, you were correct. All of my clothes are in the room with me." He held out his hand to her. "Come on, we'll find you something."

She followed him into the bedroom and stood behind him as he opened the door to the enormous walk-in closet. He entered it, flipped on the light, and grabbed a robe from a hanger on the left side. Underneath the rack of clothes, directly under the robe he'd just grabbed, was an old trunk.

He turned to hand her the robe and followed her eyes back to the floor of the closet. "What are you looking at, my dear?"

She cleared her throat. "That's a really old trunk. Was that your father's?"

He stepped out of the closet and closed the door. "Yes, as a matter of fact, it was."

She wrapped the robe around her shoulders. He didn't offer to help her; he simply watched her as she adjusted it and tied the belt.

"What do you keep in an old trunk like that?"

He left her standing in the bedroom as he walked down the hall toward the kitchen. "Nothing special, just clothes. Do you want some coffee or would you like to go back to sleep? It's pretty early, isn't it?"

She followed him into the kitchen. "I don't know what time it is. I was just a little chilly and wanted to find something warm to put on."

"Well, that robe will keep you warm." He moved the dining room curtain to the side and looked out the window. "It's still dark outside. Let's go back to bed for a few hours."

She nodded. He led her back to the bedroom and they crawled back into bed. She rested her head on his chest.

"Tell me about your father," she whispered.

"Let's sleep. I'll tell you about him tomorrow."

He kissed the top of her head and almost immediately started breathing deeply.

Penny stared at the closet door, wondering

when she would find time alone to look inside that trunk.

His voice startled her. "Forget the trunk, Penny. Go to sleep."

Jealousy and Murder

Penny woke before Levi and quietly rose from the bed to go make breakfast. She scowled at the closed closet door on her way out of the room. By the time she finished making the toast, she heard Levi in the bedroom. She placed juice and eggs on the table and was putting silverware next to the plates when he entered the dining room.

"Well, I could get used to this." He grinned as he wrapped his arm around her waist and kissed her good morning.

"Good morning, Levi. If you would like to get used to this, I suggest you hire a cook." She placed a plate of toast in the middle of the table. "Why don't you have any servants, anyway?"

He shook his head. "I never needed any." He waved his hands around the room and sat down at the table. "It's just me here. I can make my own meals and clean up after myself."

She joined him at the table. "Well, of course

you can, but why would you want to? It seems you have plenty of money to hire anyone you want."

He sipped his coffee and took a bite of fried eggs. "I never liked having too many people around. They get in my way."

"That's funny. Servants don't get in your way. They're trained to stay out of your way."

"Still, I'd rather be by myself."

Penny sipped her coffee. "Are you an only child, Levi?"

"Yes, how did you know?" He buttered his toast.

"People who don't have siblings generally like their solitude. If you've grown up with a houseful, you don't really mind having others around."

"Yet another coincidence. We're both only children."

"Well, I do have a brother, sort of. He's not really my brother but we grew up together, so I've known him since the day I was born."

"Where is he now? Home in Vicksburg?"

"I certainly hope so."

"What do you mean?" He took a bite of his toast.

"Oh, nothing, just that he has a habit of showing up sometimes."

Levi rose from the table and stepped into the kitchen to get more coffee. "If he showed up here, would he be upset about us?"

Penny didn't say anything for a moment. "Of course he wouldn't be upset, but he would be concerned about me getting hurt. He acts like a typical big brother, looking out for his little sister."

She turned to look out the dining room window

but quickly turned back to him and smiled. "I would like to run upstairs to my suite and bathe and put on some fresh clothes. Would you mind if I left?"

"Not at all. I'll wash the breakfast dishes while you're gone, seeing as I don't have a maid." He smirked.

She dressed in her clothes from the night before, returned to the kitchen, and kissed him on the cheek. "Would you like to do some hunting today?" she asked. "Nelson said the rabbits are running."

"Rabbits?"

"Yes, rabbit hunting. Do you want to go?"

"Um, I'm not sure about rabbit hunting. It seems sad to kill fuzzy little bunnies."

She walked to the front door, shaking her head. "Fuzzy bunnies?"

"Oh, I'm just kidding," he yelled after her. "Of course I'll go. It sounds like fun. Knock on the door when you're ready and we'll go." He chuckled.

She winked at him and closed the door.

***

"Where the hell have you been all night? I woke up and you weren't here. I've been pacing back and forth for hours, wondering where to look for your body."

"Luke, relax. I spent the night at Levi's."

Luke sighed. "I figured that's where you were. Why would you do that?"

"I was trying to find the trunk." She raised her eyebrows and smiled at him.

He looked questioningly back at her and she nodded.

"Really? You found it?"

"Yes! It's in his bedroom closet."

"Did you look inside?"

"No, unfortunately, he was with me the whole time. But I think I've come up with a plan. I invited him to go hunting today, so I'll leave his door ajar, and you can sneak into his apartment and get my trunk back."

"You want me to break into someone's apartment and steal something in broad daylight? If anyone sees me around here, they'll know right away I don't belong."

"No one will notice. There's a butler uniform hanging on the back of his kitchen pantry door. Put that on and if anyone asks, tell them you're Mr. Temple's new cook. No one will question it."

She skipped toward the bathroom. "Now, I have to clean up and change so I can be a good diversion."

* * *

Penny left Levi's door ajar as she promised, and she and Levi left for a day of hunting. They spent all morning and afternoon on the game preserve with guns and dogs and a guide, but for the first time, they came back empty-handed. When they returned to the annex, Penny told Levi she wanted to freshen up and would meet him in the Grand Dining Room for an early supper in an hour.

She entered her suite and found Luke sitting on the sofa. All of the curtains were drawn and he was staring into the unlit fireplace.

"Well? Where is it?" she asked, flipping on the

lights.

He looked up at her but didn't answer.

"Luke, did you find it or not?"

"I found it."

She waited but he offered no further conversation.

"Where is it?"

"I left it in his closet."

"What?! Why would you do a thing like that?"

"Penny, calm down and I'll explain."

She sat next to him on the ottoman and impatiently waited for him to explain why her trunk was still in Levi's closet.

"I found the trunk but there was a lock on it so I couldn't look inside. I moved it and indeed there is something very heavy in that trunk. So, I was going to drag it up here, but then I got to thinking. We're on an island. There's no way to get that trunk off this island unless we take it with our other suitcases on the ferry. Don't you think when you leave, he'll want to say good-bye to you and notice you're taking his trunk? I don't know what kind of plan you have to get it off the island, but I sat in the floor of his bedroom closet for an hour and couldn't come up with a single idea." He shrugged. "So, I left it...for now. At least you know where it is."

Penny was dumbstruck. Why didn't she think it through? "You're right, Luke. I was so excited to find it that I just wanted to get it back. I didn't even consider how I'd get it off the island." She looked down at the floor. "You're right about something else, too. I'll never be able to take it with me if Levi is around. I need to break it off with him so he won't see me leave with it."

Luke pulled her silk stockings from his pocket

and held them up in front of her face. "You'll probably want these back, then. They were lying on the floor of his bedroom."

Penny didn't say a word as she grabbed them from his hand.

* * *

After waiting for two hours in the Grand Dining Room for Penny to arrive, Levi gave up. He decided to walk on the beach and drown his sorrows in some alcohol. He asked the waiter for a bottle of whiskey to take with him.

"Don't you mean a glass, sir?"

"No, I don't mean a glass. I would have said 'glass' if I wanted a glass. I want a bottle. A full bottle. And I want it now."

The waiter nodded and backed up. "Yes, sir, right away."

After the man returned with a bottle, Levi took it and stomped out of the dining room. He opened it on the front steps of the club, threw his head back, and took a big swig. He sighed after he swallowed, appreciating the burn in his throat. He walked down to the beach and planned on walking for as long as his legs would carry him. He was frustrated and saddened that Penelope had stood him up. He assumed she was with someone else. Where else would she be? She had too many suitors and he was just another name in her corral. How could he have been so stupid as to let himself develop feelings for her?

The more he drank, the angrier he became, not only at himself but also at her, and by the time the bottle was half empty, he'd decided to go confront her.

He would show up at her suite and demand answers.

He stumbled down the beach, stopping every few yards to take another slug from the bottle.

"Are you all right?"

He heard a small voice coming from behind him, barely audible over the surf. He spun around and saw a young woman sitting on the sand next to some tall grasses. "Where'd you come from?"

"I was sitting here. You walked right past me." She stood, wiped the sand from her skirt, and took a couple steps toward him. "Do you need help getting home, mister? You look a little, um..."

"Drunk? Is that what you were going to say? Well, you're absolutely right. I'm drunk." He took a couple of steps toward her and stumbled. He fell down in the sand, knocking her off her feet.

Instead of being angry or embarrassed, she threw her head back and laughed. He found the tinkle of her laughter soothing. He had been so angry, but the ring of her laughter instantly lifted his spirits. They both lay on the sand and giggled for a long time. When the laughter subsided, Levi remained still and looked up at the sky. The young lady looked over at him.

"Maybe I should help you home, sir," she said as she climbed to her feet. She grabbed his arm to help him up.

"Maybe that's a good idea. I live at the annex. You want to come in with me and stay for a while?"

"Let's get you home and we'll see." She wrapped her arm around his waist and allowed him to lean on him as they zigzagged down the beach.

By the time they arrived at his apartment door, she had taken more than a few swigs from his bottle and was quite tipsy herself. She laughed hysterically as he fumbled with the lock, and she nearly fell into the door when he finally got it opened. He grabbed her elbow to keep her from falling, then dropped the empty bottle and grabbed her long blonde ponytail with his other hand. He roughly kissed her on the mouth. She didn't seem to mind, wrapping her arms around his neck. They were still kissing as he closed the door.

* * *

After the door closed, Penny emerged from her hiding place down the hall. She stomped up the stairs and slammed the door of her suite.

"Are you jealous?" Luke asked as she slammed a cabinet door in the kitchen.

"No! I'm not jealous." She slammed the teapot down on the stove.

"Now you know how I feel when you're with him."

She looked at him with her eyes wide. "What? This isn't about you, Luke. This is about the trunk."

"Then why are you so angry?"

She turned to him and placed both hands on her hips. "How can I get the trunk when he keeps a stable of drunken maids revolving through his apartment?" she snapped.

"Just calm down and have some tea. We'll find a way to get the trunk and get it off the island. But for now, relax."

Police

The morning sun was hot and bright in the eastern sky as Penny walked down the path toward the dining room for breakfast. There wasn't a cloud in the sky but the humidity was on the rise. The seabirds squawked, knowing a storm would be blowing in within hours. She was taken aback by the flurry of activity near the back kitchen door of the club, and she overhead a few of the waitresses crying and the chef trying to console them.

"Who would do something like that?" one of the girls sobbed.

"The police are here. They'll figure it out," the chef replied. "Come on, you need to pull yourself together and get back to work."

Penny walked around the building and climbed the front staircase, entering the front door without properly greeting the doorman. She marched straight down the hall to Charles's office.

"What happened now?" she asked as she

entered without knocking.

"Good morning, Miss Juzan. What are you talking about?" Charles greeted her without looking up from the papers on his desk.

"Why is the help upset? What happened?"

Charles sighed. "There was another servant girl found dead this morning. The police are handling it. That's all I know."

"What do you mean, that's all you know? Was she murdered like the others?"

"It looks that way. Now, if you'll excuse me, I have work to do."

Penny left his office and slammed the door on her way out, displaying her annoyance at being dismissed like one of the help. She walked down the hallway toward the dining room and was confronted by the sheriff.

"Oh, Miss Juzan, I'm glad you're here. I wonder if I may have a word with you," he said.

"Of course, Sheriff."

He led her to an empty room at the end of the hallway and closed the door after they entered. "Please have a seat."

"What happened, Sheriff? Was someone else killed?"

"That's exactly what I'd like to speak with you about. Another servant girl was murdered. Would you mind telling me your whereabouts last evening?"

"Of course not. I was in my suite at the annex. Why?"

"I'm just making sure everyone has an alibi, and I remember yours being a little flimsy the last two times we had incidents on the island."

"What? Are you thinking I had something to do

with these brutal murders?"

"I'm not thinking anything, ma'am, just doing my job. Now, can you tell me if anyone can corroborate your story? Did anyone see you at the annex last night?"

"Well, I...um...I don't think so." She wrinkled her brow, realizing Luke would be of no use and Levi didn't see her standing in the hallway. She gasped at the thought of Levi.

"What is it, Miss Juzan?"

"What did the victim look like?"

"About twenty, slim, long blonde hair. Why?"

"Oh, it's nothing. I thought I saw a servant girl at the annex last night, but she was a brunette, so it must have been someone else."

"All right, then. Well, you stay close in case I need to speak with you again."

"All right, Sheriff."

"I'll probably have more questions for you since you again don't have an alibi."

She huffed and left the room after the sheriff excused her. She stomped back to the annex, kicking up sand with each step, and pounded on Levi's door.

After she knocked three times, he finally opened the door. He had dark circles under his eyes and looked like he was nursing a massive hangover. "Jesus Christ, woman, are you trying to wake the dead?"

She pushed him out of the way and barged into his apartment.

"What's wrong, Penny? Why are you in such a hissy?"

"Who was that blonde girl I saw you with last night?"

He chuckled. "Oh, you're jealous. Well, if you would have shown up for our date as planned, I wouldn't have been with another girl." He didn't wait for a response. He turned from her and walked into the kitchen.

"I'm not jealous. I was just questioned at the club by the sheriff. The girl I saw you with yesterday was found this morning—murdered."

Levi stopped and turned back to her. "Murdered?"

"Yes, she's dead, Levi."

He looked down at the floor and then back at her and slowly shook his head. "What did you do, Penny?"

"What did I do? I didn't do anything. The question is, what did *you* do? Whether you know it or not, you're already suspected of killing those other two girls. Did you kill this one, too?"

He chuckled. "Oh, Penny, dear, you're so naive. If anyone is suspected of harming another on this island, it's you. You're the one with no alibis, and apparently you're the one they're questioning."

"Levi, I saw you with that girl last night."

He walked up to her and spoke in a condescending tone. "I don't think you saw anything. If you saw me, I would have seen you, too, and I didn't. Where were you, anyway?"

Penny sighed in exasperation and pointed at his face. "You're not going to get away with this." She headed for the door and then turned back toward him. "And you're certainly not going to pin it on me."

She slammed the door.

* * *

Levi quickly shaved and changed his clothes. He walked over to the club and ran into the sheriff inside the entryway.

"Mr. Temple, just the man I wanted to see."

"Good morning, Sheriff. Listen, I just had a disturbing conversation with Miss Juzan. She was very distraught that you questioned her. Did I hear her right that another girl has been murdered?"

"Yes, you heard right. Can you tell me where you were last evening?"

"Sure, I had supper here at the club, then I went for a walk down the beach and went to bed. Miss Juzan said she saw me come in but she didn't speak to me. I think she wanted me to verify her alibi but I'm afraid I can't do that. I didn't see her."

"Did you dine with anyone in particular?"

"Well, no, sir. I was supposed to have supper with Miss Juzan but she never showed up for our date." He shrugged.

"All right, Mr. Temple. Thank you for your time. I'll be in touch."

"You're welcome, Sheriff. I'll be here if you need me. Can I ask you something?"

"Sure."

"When I saw Penny, she was really furious. Why would she be so upset just because you asked her a few routine questions?"

"I'm sure I wouldn't know, Mr. Temple. Have a good day." The sheriff tipped his hat, pushed open the heavy front doors, and walked down the front steps.

Levi stepped outside and watched him walk away. He then went back inside the club and ordered a cheese omelet.

Revenge

"What's wrong now?" Luke asked when he heard Penny slam the front door.

Her face was red and her hands were fists.

"That man is absolutely infuriating!" She paced in front of the dining table.

"What man? Levi? We already knew that. What happened?"

She yanked her hat off and threw it on the table. "Another girl was murdered last night and the sheriff questioned *me* about it." She paced and shook her head. "I know Levi killed her. I saw him with her last night."

"You saw him with her? Listen, you need to stay away from that man before he hurts you, too. I think we're done here. I'm going to go pack your things and you're leaving right now."

Luke stomped down the hall toward the bedroom.

"No, Luke, stop!"

He stopped and turned around to face her.

"He's not going to murder me, but I think he is trying to frame me for these murders."

Luke walked back toward her. "How could he possibly frame you?"

"I don't know, but when I told him the girl was dead, he asked me what I did to her. I didn't do anything to her. He did. Why would he ask me that, and why would he try to pin it on me? Something strange is going on here."

Luke sighed and reached for Penny's hand. "Come sit down. We need to come up with a plan to get you off this island, with or without that trunk."

He led her to the sofa, sat her down, and told her he would make her some tea and be right back. After he disappeared into the kitchen, Penny sat silently, pondering a way to get her hands on the trunk and get it loaded onto the ferry without Levi's knowledge. She chewed on the side of her thumb as she mentally explored every possible plan, no matter how difficult or absurd it may seem. Luke returned with two cups of tea and sat down across from her. She continued thinking as she sipped the tea, staring absently at the floor.

"Penny?"

She turned toward him.

"What are you thinking?"

"I was thinking about the facts and how I can turn them into a plan. First, we know where the trunk is. Second, we know when I leave the island it has to be ferried with all my belongings. Third, we know Levi won't let that happen."

Luke took a sip of his tea. "Well, I can get the trunk for you, and you can easily get it off the island. We just need to get rid of Levi."

Penny nodded slowly. "I wonder if I can talk to the sheriff and come up with some kind of evidence that Levi killed those girls. If so, that would keep him busy with the sheriff while we make our escape."

"What kind of evidence could you come up with?"

Penny sighed and didn't answer. They both stared at the coffee table, lost in thought.

Finally Luke said, "If we can't come up with something to make the sheriff keep Levi busy, I guess I'll have to detain him myself."

"How will you do that?" Penny raised her eyebrows.

"You leave that to me. Just pack your bags tonight and get ready to go."

Lori Crane

Kidnapped

Late that evening, Levi returned home from dining at the club. When he put the key in the lock and turned, something was amiss. He usually heard a clicking sound as the mechanism moved, but this time there was no sound. He slowly turned the knob and opened the door an inch. He reached his hand inside the door, relocked it, and closed it to try again. He inserted his key and turned. *Click.* There was the sound. He paused a moment and then shrugged. He wasn't sure he had locked it when he went to the dining room, or perhaps his mind was otherwise occupied and he simply didn't hear the sound the first time.

He entered the apartment and closed the door, flipped on the light switch and looked around the room. Nothing was out of place. He kicked off his shoes and pushed them under the dining room table. He removed his jacket and hung it on the back of the chair. He then pulled his belt from its loops and laid it across the top of his jacket. He yawned and realized he was dead tired. He wanted nothing more than to collapse in his bed and allow sweet sleep to carry him away.

When he entered his bedroom door, he reached to his right for the light switch. As his fingers made contact with it, something sharp struck the back of his head. He thought his temples would explode from the pain as he collapsed onto his knees. He continued falling forward, unable to stop the momentum, and landed painfully on his face. As his cheekbone hit the wooden floor, he heard a footstep behind him. He lay on his stomach and turned his head in the direction of the footstep, and though his vision was blurring, he saw a worn brown boot. A man's boot. He rolled his eyes up to see the face of his assailant, but as he tried to bring the shadowy figure into focus, everything went black.

Word from the Artist

Penny was sitting alone in the sunny Grand Dining Room, sipping orange juice, when she saw Charles nearly running toward Nelson's table. She watched the two have an animated conversation. She could hear their voices but couldn't make out what they were saying. She heard Charles say something about New York. His face was red with anger and his fists were clenched at his sides. She could see his temples pulsing from halfway across the room. After he spoke to Nelson, Nelson's face went pale. Charles turned and stomped away, and Nelson hastily pushed his chair back from the table and jumped up to follow him.

When she turned to watch their hurried departure, she saw them bump into the sheriff in the doorway. As usual, the man held his hat by the brim and was spinning it around. The trio talked for a moment. What in the world had Charles so upset? Whatever it was had also shocked Nelson, but while Charles spoke to the sheriff, there was no expression whatsoever on the sheriff's face. He remained poised and maintained eye contact with Charles, but did begin to spin his hat faster than normal. The men turned and disappeared from the doorway.

Penny decided to follow them.

The waiter approached her table and placed pancakes in front of her. "Can I get you more orange juice, ma'am, or perhaps some coffee?"

"No, I've lost my appetite." She almost knocked him out of the way as she quickly rose to her feet.

He awkwardly stepped aside. "Is there something wrong, ma'am?"

She shook her head and thrust her linen napkin in his hand. "No. I have to go."

She left him standing at the table holding her napkin as she scurried to the doorway and peeked around the corner. The men were rounding the next corner into the hallway that led to Charles's office. She followed.

She stood at the end of the hallway until she heard the office door close. She crouched a bit and tiptoed across the parquet floor, but she realized she probably looked ridiculous. It was the middle of the morning; no one would question why she was in the hallway. She stood up straight, smoothed down her dress, and walked normally toward the office door. When she reached it, she leaned her back against the wall so her ear was right at the crack of the door. If anyone witnessed her in the hallway, she would say Charles was in a meeting and she was waiting for him. She slowed her breathing and listened.

"I heard from him this morning," said Charles.

"Are you sure this is the correct artist?" Nelson

asked.

"Yes, Arthur Bowen Davies from New York. He has done many paintings for Cornelius."

"So, what's the problem?" asked the sheriff.

Charles's voice rose in frustration. "None of them was procured by Mr. Temple."

There was silence for a moment.

Nelson asked, "So, what did he have to say about Levi?"

"He didn't have anything to say about him. He's never met Levi Temple. He's never even heard of Levi Temple."

"Do you think Mr. Temple is a fraud?" asked the sheriff.

"Not only do I think he's a fraud, Sheriff, I think he may be our murderer," Charles stated.

"Why would you think that?"

"Because no one has ever been attacked or murdered on this island until Levi Temple showed up. If he is the fraud I now know he is, then why not be the murderer in our midst also?"

"I have narrowed the murderer down to the newcomers, Levi Temple and Penelope Juzan, but I don't think a woman of her petite stature would have the strength to murder those girls the way they were murdered. I've been leaning toward Mr. Temple for quite some time. I just haven't found the proof to arrest him."

"What's our next step?" Nelson asked.

"Do you know where we might find Mr. Temple?" the sheriff asked.

"I haven't seen him around this morning," Nelson answered. "He may still be in his apartment...well, Cornelius's apartment."

"Let me round up a deputy and head over there to have a chat with him. Do me a favor and leave him alone until I have the chance to speak with him."

Penny placed her hand over her agape mouth. She knew Levi was a fraud and probably a murderer, but to hear someone else confirm it was frightening. She had been alone with him numerous times, and she wondered if she had ever been in danger on any of those occasions. One thing she knew for sure—she needed to get that trunk out of his closet before the sheriff searched the apartment.

She heard footsteps coming toward the door and quickly ran down the hall. She ran down the front steps of the club and headed straight to Levi's apartment.

Evidence

Penny had barely gotten the trunk to the top of the stairs when she heard the sheriff and his deputy enter the building. She was sweating head to toe from dragging it all the way up the stairs Luke was right when he said it was heavy. It took every ounce of strength and willpower she had to get it to the top of the steps. She pulled it in the door of her suite and left it sitting in the middle of the living room and closed the door. She wiped the sweat from her upper lip and tucked her hair into its pin before descending the stairs to greet the sheriff.

"Sheriff? Is that you?"

"Good morning, Miss Juzan." He removed his hat and spun it.

"Can I help you with something?"

"No, ma'am. We're here to speak with Mr. Temple."

"Oh, I haven't seen him this morning."

"That's all right, ma'am. We'll find him. If you'll

excuse me, I have work to do." He turned and walked away from her.

"Oh, certainly, Sheriff. I didn't mean to detain you," she said sweetly.

"It's no problem, ma'am."

She turned around and took a few steps back up to her suite, but she paused on the landing to listen to the men. They knocked on the door a few times, then the sheriff told his deputy to break the door down.

"No need to, Sheriff. It's unlocked."

"Oh, well, what are you waiting for?"

The men left the door open and Penny crept down to the hallway to listen to their conversation.

"Take a look around and don't skip anything. Check every nook and cranny," ordered the sheriff.

"What exactly are we looking for?"

"Anything one would use to strangle a girl."

Penny peeked inside and saw the deputy next to a dining room chair, bent over, digging through the pockets of Levi's jacket. He froze with one hand in a pocket, his nose only inches from the belt that lay across the jacket. He slowly stood up and rubbed his hand across the belt. "What about a belt, Sheriff?"

The sheriff emerged from the kitchen and Penny quickly moved her head out of the doorway to avoid being seen. She held her breath.

"A belt?"

"Yes, there's one here on the chair. It has some sort of Indian design on it."

"Indian design?"

"Yes, Sheriff, look."

There was silence for a moment.

"I'll be damned," muttered the sheriff. "These are the same markings that were found on all three of the victims' throats. It looks like we've found our murderer."

Penny didn't need to hear anymore. She tiptoed down the hall and climbed the stairs to her suite. She was panting by the time she closed her door. She stood with her back against it, trying to catch her breath. Her suspicions were true. Levi was the killer.

From directly behind her head, there was a knock on the door. She jumped. She looked around the room and saw the trunk in the middle of the floor. A second knock. She didn't have time to move the trunk; there was nothing she could do. If Levi was at the door, he would see the trunk and probably murder her next. No, it couldn't be Levi. The sheriff would have seen him enter the building. A third knock.

Then a small voice from the other side of the door. "Miss Juzan?"

A child's voice.

She slowly turned the knob and cracked open the door.

It was a young boy.

"Miss Juzan?"

"Yes?"

He held up a folded piece of paper. "This is for you."

She cautiously reached for it while the boy watched her.

"I'm supposed to let you read it, then take your luggage to the dock."

"Oh." She unfolded the paper. It was not signed but was in Luke's handwriting.

He is detained. Send your things to the dock right now and leave in the morning.

She looked back at the boy. "Give me a few minutes to finish packing."

The boy nodded.

Luke

Levi was groggy when he woke, and felt a throbbing pain on the back of his head and a horrible ache on his right cheek. He stretched open his jaw which made his cheek ache even worse. He tried to touch it but his arms wouldn't move. His wrists were bound behind his back, tied to something. He struggled against the binding but it was too tight. He blinked, attempting to bring his vision into focus, and looked around the dim room. The evening sun blazed behind the single curtain to his right. It gave the room a reddish tinge. He scanned his surroundings and didn't recognize anything. Where was he? How did he get here?

There was a small wooden table with three chairs in the corner. He looked down at his seat. He was sitting in the fourth chair. The backs of the chairs were made of spindles. He pulled at his ties again; he must've been tied to the spindles. The floor was scraped wooden plank and the walls were made of logs. A log cabin? He rubbed his foot across the wood and realized he wasn't wearing any shoes. What happened to his shoes? There was a soot-covered stone fireplace to his left that looked like it hadn't been lit in years. No wood was stacked beside it, but a poker covered in cobwebs leaned against the side. To his right was a wooden door. There was nothing else in the room. He tried to stand but couldn't. He looked back over his shoulder to see what lay behind him, but his head exploded with pain when he moved. He groaned.

"Oh, you're awake." A man's voice came from behind him, monotone with a touch of Southern accent. Levi had never heard the voice before.

"Where am I?" Levi asked, his dry throat making his voice sound like a croak.

The man laughed. "I'd like to tell you you're in Hell where you belong, but we're not that lucky, are we?"

"Who are you?"

"Let's just say I'm a friend."

"You're no friend of mine."

"I didn't say *your* friend."

Levi heard footsteps as the man slowly approached him, walked around him, and stopped about five feet in front of him. He had black hair and black eyes. An Indian. He wore a wrinkled blue shirt and worn brown boots. Instantly Levi's mind flooded with the memory of the surprise attack in his apartment.

"You're the one who hit me."

"I had to get you here and I didn't think you'd come along peacefully. You should have seen yourself draped over the donkey with your face hanging in his butt. It was quite a sight." The man smiled.

"Where am I?"

"Oh, you're still on the island, but no one will ever venture way out here to look for you."

"What do you want? Why do you have me tied up?"

"I need you to stay put for a little while. I'm not sure what we'll do with you after that."

"After what? And who's 'we'?"

"You ask far too many questions. I don't know what she sees in you."

"She?"

The Indian turned away and Levi saw the pearl handle of Penny's pistol sticking out of the man's waistband.

"Penny? Where is she? If you hurt her, I swear I'll kill you." He struggled against his bindings but couldn't move his wrists without the ropes cutting into them.

The Indian turned back to Levi and laughed. "I wouldn't hurt Penny. It seems you're the one on the island who murders people." He paused for a moment, then his face transformed into a sincere look. "Why haven't you killed her yet?"

"Killed who? Penny? Why would I kill Penny? What are you talking about?"

"Well, we'll just wait for a while and see what happens, shall we?"

The Indian walked out the front door, leaving Levi alone to imagine his fate.

The Truth

Penny finished packing her belongings and sent them with the boy to the ferry dock. Her luggage amounted to three suitcases—one belonging to Luke—and two trunks—one formerly belonging to Levi Temple. It was still locked so she hadn't been able to look inside, but it was so heavy, she knew it held a great amount of treasure. She would worry about removing the lock once she safely got it off the island.

She decided to borrow a horse from the stable and go out to the hunting shack on the other side of the island. Luke would be holding Levi there and she wanted to tell him what had happened with Charles and Nelson and what the sheriff had found in Levi's apartment. She also wanted to plan a place for them to meet once they were both on the mainland.

In the late afternoon, she rode out to the shack and passed what used to be George Turner's place. She stopped the horse and looked down at the black rubble left by the fire. She dismounted and walked among the debris.

"Poor George. What in the world happened to your beautiful home?"

The brick chimney was the only thing left of the house. She kicked over a charred log that rested in front of it. Maybe the log had fallen out of the fireplace and was the reason for the fire. Underneath the log was something shiny. She stooped, picked it up, and wiped it off on the sleeve of her coat. One side was black with soot, the other had been protected by the log and flashed silver through the grime. She recognized the fish-scale design.

"You son of a..."

She tucked it in her pocket and quickly remounted her horse. She kicked him in the ribs and galloped toward the shack.

By the time she arrived at the other side of the island, it was almost dusk. The shack looked dark and foreboding. The single window in front was not illuminated by any light. She tiptoed up the stone step and slowly opened the squeaking wooden door.

Levi spun his head to the right when he heard the door and saw her standing there. "Penny? Oh, thank God you found me. Untie these ropes and let's get out of here."

Penny cocked her head to the right and smiled. "Now why would I do that, Levi?"

Levi looked dumbfounded. "Why wouldn't you? The Indian man who kidnapped me has your pistol. I thought he hurt you. Thank God you're all right."

She slowly walked toward him and stood staring at him, surprised that he didn't seem to know what was going on. "I'm glad I have your undivided attention,

Levi. I have a few things to say to you."

He looked puzzled. "Please untie me."

"No, not yet." She removed her gloves and set them on the table. "First, let's talk about today's events." She pulled a chair from the table, blew the dust off of it, and set it directly in front of Levi. "I was at the club and heard Charles and Nelson saying they got word from that artist in New York."

"So?"

"So, it seems that artist has never heard of you. Are you surprised?"

Levi didn't answer.

"Of course you're not. You've never met the man, have you?"

They stared at each other for a moment.

Penny broke the silence. "Then guess what happened? They told the sheriff to find you so they could throw you off the island, but you were nowhere to be found. The sheriff and his deputy searched your apartment and guess what they found there?"

She paused for dramatic effect.

"They found your belt. The belt with the same markings on it as those on the murdered girls' throats. Isn't that interesting?"

"Penny, I don't know what you're talking about. Untie me, please."

"All right, one more thing." She reached into her pocket and pulled out the silver lighter she had retrieved from George Turner's house. "Do you recognize this?"

"Yes. Where did you find it?"

She laughed a deep belly laugh. "Well, where was the last place you used it?" She looked at the confusion on his face. "Maybe at George Turner's house? You set that fire and you killed poor Mr. Turner. I would say that I was deeply saddened by his demise, but the truth is I hardly knew him."

"I set that fire for you, Penny. I saw you with George and it sent me into a jealous rage." He looked down at the floor like a child who was embarrassed after being caught doing something wrong. "I think I'm in love with you, Penny."

Luke slammed the door and Levi jerked his head up, wide eyed, looking at Luke then at Penny. Luke walked up to her and kissed her on the cheek. Penny smiled at him.

"Wait, you're in on this? You know him?" Levi asked.

"Remember I told you I had a brother? I'm surprised you didn't figure it out sooner."

Luke lit a lantern and set it on the table.

Penny continued, "I'll tell you what, I was simply going to leave the island without seeing you again, but after finding your lighter at George's house and remembering how you were trying to frame me for the murders of those girls, I decided to come out and talk to you first."

"I don't know what you're up to, but I can pay you whatever you want. I'll pay you to let me go."

Penny and Luke looked at each other.

"Levi, you can't pay me anything because you're broke." Penny smirked.

"I'm not broke. I have a whole trunk of gold. I can get it for you."

"I'm sorry. That trunk isn't in your closet anymore. It's already at the dock being loaded onto the ferry with the rest of my belongings."

"What?"

Penny turned to Luke. "Would you mind excusing us for a few minutes? We have some unfinished business to discuss."

Luke nodded and exited through the front door.

Penny took a seat on the chair in front of Levi. "I would apologize for taking the trunk, but it's not really yours, is it?"

"Of course it's mine."

She narrowed her eyes. "Tell me about Carter Stuckey"

Even in the dim lamplight, Penny could see Levi's face turn ashen.

She repeated her question. "Carter Stuckey? That name ring a bell?"

"What do you know about Carter Stuckey?"

"I know he was supposed to deliver a trunk to my father in Vicksburg and he never showed up. After my mother died, I inherited my great-grandfather's journal. The last four or five entries were written in my father's handwriting. It told the story of the trunk and that Carter Stuckey had retrieved it from our lake, and he had sent word to my father that it would arrive within the week, but we never saw it...or him."

She rose and paced back and forth in front of Levi as she continued her story.

"I tracked down the last place where Carter Stuckey was seen and it was in Lauderdale County, Mississippi. So, I went there and spoke with the sheriff. Sadly, he confirmed that Carter Stuckey was one of the victims of a brutal murderer who owned an inn located on the banks of Chunky River."

Levi watched her as she paced in front of him. He sat as still as stone and didn't say a word.

"This happened over ten years ago, back in

1901. You know what else the sheriff told me? He said the killer had a son who was about twelve at the time. He was a blond waif by the name of Levi, and when his father was hung for murder, the boy up and disappeared without a trace. The funny part about the story is that the sheriff's name was Temple—J.R. Temple. Just like your surname. Isn't that funny?"

She stopped in front of him and bent over, her lips only inches from his face.

"Is any of this making sense to you, Mr. Temple? Or should I call you Levi Stuckey?"

He looked at her with hatred and a heaping tablespoon of fear. She looked back at him with the slightest smile playing on her lips.

"What do you want?" he muttered.

She stood up straight. "Oh, I already got what I want. I got my family's property back. That trunk belonged to my father and his father before him and his father before him. You see, Levi, that trunk was not yours for the taking. Though you think you deserve so much, you don't deserve that. But I will tell you a secret. Before I board the ferry in the morning, I'll let the Charles know where to find you. I'm sure he'll be only too happy to release you from these ropes. He'll have the sheriff take you to the mainland and you'll finally get everything you so deserve."

The Curse

Penny walked out of the shack and found Luke leaning against a moss-draped oak, chewing on a long blade of grass. The moon had begun its rise and the sun filtered its last rays of light, leaving a pink tinge in the sky.

"Well?" Luke inquired.

"I said what I had to say to him. You can do whatever you want with him now."

"What do you want me to do with him?"

"I don't really care. I got what I came here for. I told him the sheriff would come release him tomorrow. I didn't say whether the sheriff would find him alive or dead."

"I'm not going to kill him, Penny. Why don't I just wait until you're off the island then let him go?"

"No!" she snapped. "You can't let him go. He's murdered at least four people we know of. He'll come looking for me—for us. He needs to be turned over to the sheriff or dumped in the swamp. Your choice."

Luke looked down and shuffled his boots on

the sandy ground. An owl hooted in the distance, announcing nightfall would soon be upon them. They both looked in the direction of the sound.

"So, what are we going to do now?" he asked, staring off into the darkening treetops.

"I guess we'll head back to Vicksburg and see if I can buy back the plantation."

"Do you think you can?"

"I don't know, but it's worth a try. I can certainly offer them a handsome price."

"What if the gold really does have a curse on it?"

"Don't be silly. Nothing bad is going to happen. There's no such thing as curses. It's an old wives' tale—family folklore."

Luke tossed the blade of grass away and shook his head. "Penny, our great-grandfathers were the best of friends until that trunk of gold tore them apart. They both drowned in Lake Juzan because of that trunk."

"That was forever ago and both of their deaths were mishaps. Daddy said Grandpa Pierre wasn't a very good swimmer. That's why he drowned. And he said your great-grandpa Leon died from an accident."

"You think so? What about their sons, our grandfathers? They both died for that gold, too."

"Really, Luke! Gabriel Juzan died of a snakebite and Martin Fisher died of heatstroke. Aren't you being a little gullible believing in curses?"

"I don't think so. We've always known they all died in the lake, but I always thought the circumstances were too coincidental. While reading the journals, all the pieces suddenly fit together and I don't think they were coincidences anymore. Our ancestors died on Lake Juzan searching for that gold."

She didn't say anything.

"What about your father?" Luke continued. "He collapsed of a heart attack the very same day he got the message that Carter Stuckey was on his way to Vicksburg with the trunk."

"Don't bring my father into this! He had a weak heart. That had nothing to do with the gold." She turned and looked down the path at the horse she had ridden in on.

Luke raised his voice. "Penny, it had everything to do with the gold. Your father never had a weak heart. He was the strongest man I've ever known."

She spun around and glared at him. He had never raised his voice to her and his anger surprised them both. They stopped speaking and Penny looked at the ground, caught in the painful memory of losing her father.

"What about Carter Stuckey?" Luke broke the silence.

"What about him?

"He too died with that gold in his possession."

"Really, Luke. He was murdered. That wasn't an accident and had nothing to do with the lake or the trunk."

"Well, after he died, Levi's father was in possession of the gold. What happened to him?"

"He was hung for murder."

"See? And then where did the gold go?"

"Levi's had it all this time."

"And what do you think is going to happen to him? They'll hang him or he'll rot in jail. Either way, his life is ruined, and it's all because of the gold."

"They're just coincidences, Luke. Nothing like that is going to happen to me." She took a step toward her horse.

"Penny," he said softly. "There's something you don't know."

"What?" She stopped and faced him.

"My mother told me a story and made me vow to never tell a soul, but I think it's time you know the truth.

"After my great-grandfather Leon drowned in the lake, my great-grandmother Eula got into a fight with your great-grandfather Pierre. She blamed him for her husband's death. My mother said the two had a heated argument and Pierre struck her and screamed at her to mind her own business or get off his land. She was a full-blooded Choctaw from the nearby village of Chanki Chitto and she had nowhere to go. A few years before, her entire family had relocated to Oklahoma following the signing of the Treaty of Dancing Rabbit Creek. Nearly all of the Choctaw had left, including every member of Eula's family. Eula didn't go with them because she was in love with Leon. They had a son, my grandfather Martin, and had made a life for themselves in Lauderdale County. Great-grandpa Leon was also a Choctaw, but he had been at Pierre's side for over thirty years. They built an inn and tavern and went into business together. They both took wives and had sons. Pierre was good to Leon and Eula for a very long time, until Pierre and Leon they got this idea to rob a passing coach carrying a trunk of gold. They chased the coach and the horses came unhitched and it crashed into the lake. The drivers were murdered and the coach rolled over a bluff and sank into the lake. Great-grandpa Leon died trying to fish the trunk out of the water. Pierre watched him drown and didn't save him. Great-grandma Eula was furious with Pierre for allowing it to happen.

"As he stomped away, he pushed her aside and she fell and broke her arm. He didn't stop to help her. She vowed to make him pay—for his horrible treatment of her, and for her husband's death. She vowed to never let him get his hands on that gold, and she went out to the lake that evening under the full moon. She waded through the grasses that grew tall around the lake. She lit a candle and placed it on a piece of bark and floated it across the surface of the water. She called forth the snakes, the moon, and the deep, cold water to exact revenge on Pierre Juzan and his precious gold. The candle floated out to the middle of the lake. She spoke in her native Indian tongue and placed a curse on the trunk, the gold, and anyone who holds it in their possession. The candle spun around in the middle of the lake, clouds blew in from the west, thunder rumbled from the heavens, and lightning burst forth from the sky and struck the candle. It exploded and sank into the murky depths.

"Ever since then, anyone who has tried to retrieve the gold from the lake or been in possession of it has died a horrible death. I know you don't believe in curses, but I know the gold is cursed, because my great-grandmother is the one who put the curse on it."

The sky was now black and the owl hooted again in the trees as Luke finished his story. Penny stared at him for a long time before she finally said, "Well, if we don't have the gold, then we can't buy back the plantation and we have nothing. If your family put the curse on it, then you need to find a way to take the curse off it."

"I don't know how to remove a curse."

"I suggest you find a way." She pulled her wrap

tightly around her shoulders and headed toward her sleeping horse. "I'm going to be on the ferry *with* the gold first thing in the morning. Before I go, I'm going to leave a message for Charles and the sheriff and let them know where to find Levi. You need to be gone by the time they get here. I'll meet you at the hotel next to the train station in Birmingham as soon as you can sneak off the island. I'll wait for you."

Levi's Demise

Early the following morning, Charles entered the club and was immediately handed an envelope by the doorman. The front read MR. CHARLES LANIER. He walked down the long hallway to his office, sat behind his desk, and opened the mysterious envelope. Inside was a single piece of paper with the following note.

If you would like to bring your murderer to justice, he will be waiting for you in the old hunting shack on the far side of the island, just past the game preserve. He is tied up and won't be going anywhere. He also admitted to murdering George Turner by burning his house down with the enclosed lighter. Your assumptions that he is not who he claims to be are correct. You know him as Levi Temple but his real name is Levi Stuckey. He is the son of a murderer. If you'd like to know more about him, contact J.R. Temple, the retired sheriff of Lauderdale County, Mississippi. Sheriff Temple has been searching for Levi Stuckey for ten years and will be happy to tell you all about him.

Charles emptied the contents of the envelope into his palm and examined the charred silver lighter, turning it over and over again in his hand. It was mostly covered with black soot, but he could make out an embossed design that looked like fish scales.

He returned to the entry and asked the doorman where the envelope had come from. The doorman said it was handed to him by a young boy who had darted off as soon as the envelope exchanged hands. Charles asked the doorman to send someone for the sheriff immediately.

When the sheriff arrived, Charles showed him the letter and the lighter and they took a wagon out to the hunting shack.

They entered the shack, guns drawn, and found Levi exactly as the letter had promised. The sheriff approached Levi, but Charles remained standing in the doorway.

Levi looked up when he heard the door creak open. "Thank God you found me, Sheriff!"

"Well, you're exactly where they said you'd be."

"Where who said? Did you find Penny?"

"Penny? What about Penny?"

"She's the one who kidnapped me."

"Penelope Juzan kidnapped you?" The sheriff chuckled. "She's only a tiny woman. She couldn't possibly kidnap a fully grown man."

"Well, it wasn't actually her who grabbed me and brought me here. It was that Indian."

"What Indian? There aren't any Indians on the island."

"Yes, she has a friend who's an Indian."

"What's this Indian's name?"

"I don't know. They never said. Where's

Penny?"

"I'm afraid she's gone from the island."

"Did she take my trunk? She stole an old trunk from me."

"I don't know anything about an old trunk. What was in this alleged trunk?"

"Um, just stuff, you know, some rare art, some gold pieces."

The sheriff shook his head. "Sorry, can't help you." He grabbed a chair from the table and faced the back of it toward Levi. He sat down backward and rested his arms across the top of it. "Why don't we start from the beginning? What's your real name, Mr. Temple?"

"Oh, come on, Sheriff, you know my name is Levi Temple."

"Well, then, who is Levi Stuckey?"

Levi went pale.

"All right, I'll ask one more time. What is your real name?"

Levi's face turned from white to red as his anger grew. "You know my name and I would appreciate it if you would untie me and go after my kidnappers."

"Miss Juzan and an unnamed Indian fellow?"

Levi sighed.

"Mr. Temple or Stuckey, whatever your name is, tell me—where are you from?"

"I live in New York."

"Where were you born?"

"Why all the questions? Can you please untie me?" He struggled against his bindings.

"All in good time. Were you born in Lauderdale County?"

"Yes, yes, I was. Now untie me!"

"A few more questions, if you don't mind." The sheriff pulled a brown leather belt from his jacket pocket. "Do you recognize this belt?"

"Yes, it's mine."

The sheriff looked down at it. "Interesting design it has on it. Do you know that's the same design as the markings found on the murdered girls' throats?"

"What? I don't know what you're talking about," Levi stopped struggling and sat still.

The sheriff reached into his other pocket and pulled out the lighter. "Do you recognize this?"

"Yes, that's mine, too, but I haven't seen it for quite some time."

"Since you burnt down George Turner's house?"

"What? I never burned down anyone's house. Penny and that Indian are trying to set me up. They're trying to frame me. They stole my lighter and my belt and kidnapped me and tied me up here in this shack. I thought I was going to die here."

"Well, you'll probably still die but it won't be here. It'll be from hanging."

The sheriff stood up, walked around behind Levi, and untied him from the chair but kept Levi's hands bound together. The sheriff pulled him to his feet. "Levi, you are under arrest for the murder of three servant girls and George Turner, and for the arson of George Turner's house."

Charles and the sheriff placed Levi in the back of the wagon and drove him directly to the ferry dock.

* * *

Penny watched from behind the corner of the Mainland General Store as the sheriff carted a shoeless Levi from the ferry to a waiting wagon and hauled him off to jail.

When they were out of sight, she climbed onto her own wagon and clicked her tongue at the horses. She glanced over her shoulder and admired the old trunk in the back of her wagon, wondering what it would take to break that lock. She rode west into the afternoon sun on her way to Birmingham, where she would wait for Luke to meet her. After a long year of searching, she'd finally found her treasure. She knew there was no curse, and she was certain her father would be proud of her.

The End

Author's Notes

I grew up in Lauderdale County, Mississippi, and heard the legends surrounding Stuckey's Bridge throughout my childhood. Stuckey's Bridge is located in Meehan, Mississippi, and has long been the product of curious ghost hunters and weekend six packs. I couldn't resist creating the story of the man behind the legend. It became *The Legend of Stuckey's Bridge*. While writing that book, I created Levi Stuckey/Temple, and received numerous e-mails and messages asking me about Levi's past. Though I'm sure his childhood was very interesting, I was more compelled to tell his adult story. Although he's fictional, the time and setting of this story is historically accurate.

Many thanks go out to family, friends, and associates who provided invaluable support as this book was written:

Elyse Dinh-McCrillis: TheEditNinja.com
Jen Quist: JenQPhotography.com
Robert Hess: book designer

About the Author

Lori Crane was born in Meridian, Mississippi, and now lives in greater Nashville, Tennessee. She is a member of the Daughters of the American Revolution, the United Daughters of the Confederacy, and the United States Daughters of 1812. She is a professional musician and a member of the Screen Actors Guild-American Federation of Radio and Television Artists.

Books by Lori Crane

Okatibbee Creek Series

Okatibbee Creek
An Orphan's Heart
Elly Hays

Stuckey's Bridge Trilogy

The Legend of Stuckey's Bridge
Stuckey's Legacy: The Legend Continues
Stuckey's Gold: The Curse of Lake Juzan

Culpepper Saga

I, John Culpepper
John Culpepper the Merchant
John Culpepper, Esquire
Culpepper's Rebellion

Other Titles by Lori Crane

Savannah's Bluebird
Witch Dance
The Culpepper-Fairfax Scandal
On This Day: A Perpetual Calendar for Family Genealogy

For more information, please visit
www.LoriCrane.com
or e-mail LoriCraneAuthor@gmail.com